Dear reader,

Please find enclosed your pass to BADNESS.

Being bad is a <u>choice</u>. Don't be bad all of the time, please. But do read on if you want to learn how to be a *true* villain.

P.S. Sorry, adults . . .

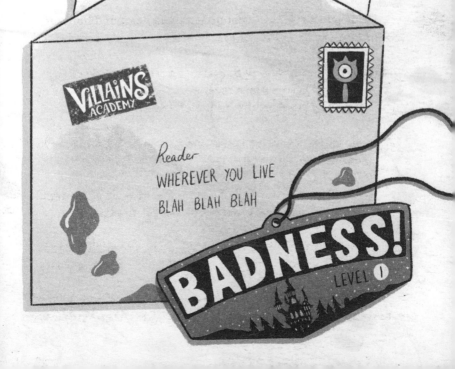

Villains ACADEMY

Reader
WHEREVER YOU LIVE
BLAH BLAH BLAH

BADNESS!
LEVEL 1

PROPERTY OF
Sheila x

First published in Great Britain in 2023 by Simon & Schuster UK Ltd

Copyright © 2023 Ryan Hammond

*So don't thin[k]
about it or
ELSE!*

The right of Ryan Hammond to be identified as the author and illustrator
of this work has been asserted by him in accordance with sections 77
and 78 of the Copyright, Designs and Patents Act, 1988.

1 3 5 7 9 10 8 6 4 2

Simon & Schuster UK Ltd
1st Floor, 222 Gray's Inn Road
London WC1X 8HB

www.simonandschuster.co.uk
www.simonandschuster.com.au
www.simonandschuster.co.in

Simon & Schuster Australia, Sydney
Simon & Schuster India, New Delhi

A CIP catalogue record for this book
is available from the British Library.

PB ISBN 978-1-3985-1461-4
eBook ISBN 978-1-3985-1462-1
eAudio ISBN 978-1-3985-1463-8

VERY
NAUGHTY
VILLAINS

Printed and bound by CPI Group (UK) Ltd,
Croydon, CR0 4YY

*Though I, Sheila,
am VERY real.*

SEE

*No, I
DONT!!*

FSC
MIX
Paper | Supporting
responsible forestry
FSC® C171272

BRAN
MASTER
MARDYBUM

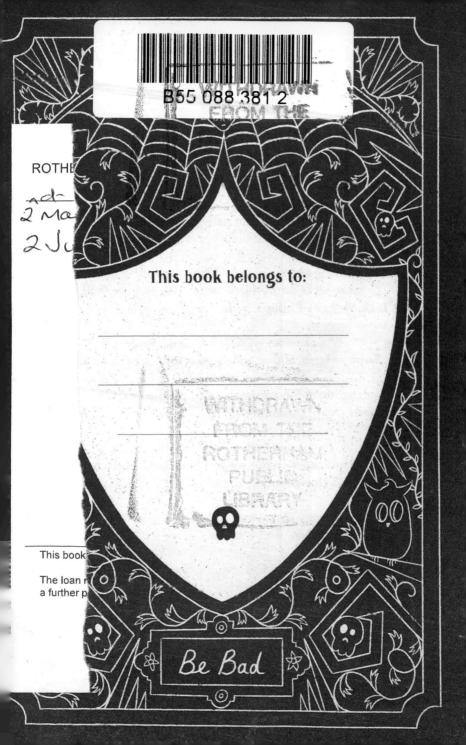

This book belongs to:

Be Bad

PRAISE FOR VILLAINS ACADEMY

VILLAINS ACADEMY

Written, illustrated and designed by

RYAN HAMMOND

SIMON AND SCHUSTER

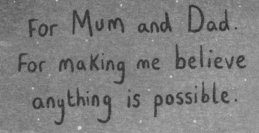

For Mum and Dad.
For making me believe
anything is possible.

X

CHAPTER 1

HOW TO BE BAD

Master Mardybum's enormous sleeves billowed through the air as he entered the classroom, his eyes burning red. 'Welcome, Class Z, to Villains Academy – the most prestigious villain school in the entire land. You'll either leave here as a fully formed villain . . . or in *tatters*.'

Bram watched the teacher in awe as sparks shot from his fingertips. Master Mardybum had been one of the most notorious villains back in the day. There were rumours that he had conquered entire cities, destroyed heroes in the blink of an eye and even flushed his arch nemesis' head down the toilet. Bram hoped that one day he could be a smidgen as bad as Master Mardybum.

'OH, BUMBERSHINS!'

Bram exclaimed, frantically searching through his bag.

'Excuse me?' Master Mardybum scowled. 'What did you just call me?'

'Nothing, sir,' Bram said, growing hot and flustered. 'I . . . I can't find my pen.'

'Likely excuse,' said the

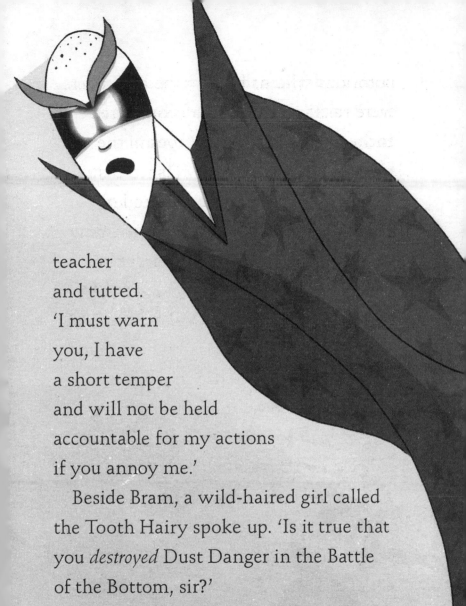

teacher
and tutted.
'I must warn
you, I have
a short temper
and will not be held
accountable for my actions
if you annoy me.'

Beside Bram, a wild-haired girl called
the Tooth Hairy spoke up. 'Is it true that
you *destroyed* Dust Danger in the Battle
of the Bottom, sir?'

The teacher grinned, not even
attempting to hide his pride. 'All in good

time. And it was the Battle of the *Bootom*, not Bottom. It's a wonderfully dark forest in the depths of Ick. I'll tell you about it one day . . . maybe. Now, back to the lesson. Over the next year, I'm going to teach you everything you need to know about being *bad*. I'm a big believer in hands-on activities to give you the best chance of surviving as a villain in the big wide world.'

The students watched in wonder. A boy with screws in his head wrote down notes eagerly. A toad in a top hat scratched his tummy, looking bored.

And in the corner, at the back of the room, a humongous lion *snored*.

Bram felt the pit of his stomach tingle with first-day nerves and he began to wonder what he'd let himself in for. His mind spun with doubts. Would he ever be bad enough to graduate Villains Academy? And if he did, would he be able to get a job in the real world as a villain when there were so many others to compete with?

He looked around at the eclectic mix of animals, humans, elves and all-round awful creatures. They burped, hissed and

radiated badness without even trying. And the worst part of all was that every one of them was likely to destroy Bram as easily as Master Mardybum had destroyed Dust Danger with his . . . bottom, was it?

'You've been accepted into this school to train as villains,' Master Mardybum continued. 'You're all young, so there's time to whip you into shape, even if your skills are still . . . basic. Now, you there, toad face. Tell me, what's the *baddest* thing you've ever done?'

'I ate a child,'

the toad said in a *tremendously* posh accent. 'It was making too much noise and I *hate* noise. So I swallowed it whole. Though I did eventually spit it back out

covered in slime. I'm not a total monster.'
A wicked smile split his face.

'Excellent! Children are the *worst*,'
Master Mardybum agreed. 'Oi, you,
Bryan the sleepy lion! What's the baddest
thing you've ever done?'

The lion stirred slightly and cracked
open one eye. His head was ginormous
and covered with fluffy auburn hair.

He looked quite friendly until he flashed his sharp teeth in a large yawn. Everyone waited expectantly for his reply, but he didn't say a word. Instead, he lifted his tail, let out a loud fart and went back to sleep.

'Interesting.' Master Mardybum nodded and swiftly moved away from the smell. Beside Bryan, a cat and a crocodile shuffled their desks away whilst covering their noses. 'You, Frankenstein, what's the worst thing you've ever done?'

'Actually, my name is Mal,' the boy with stitches in his pale face replied with a frown. 'I stole my grandma's teeth.'

'Fantastic!' Master Mardybum exclaimed. 'What a brilliant bunch of trainee villains we have this year. What about you, werewolf?'

Bram felt like a hundred pairs of eyes were watching him.

He didn't have strong muscles or an evil mind, and he certainly wasn't a terrifying lion. His fur was pale green and covered his whole body. Apparently it was supposed to glow in the dark on a full moon, which was when he was meant to feel the most powerful and BAD, but that had never happened in his entire life. As Bram was always in wolf form, his parents assumed that he'd be *extra* bad. But he wasn't. His claws were small and cared for. His teeth were clean and bright. He wasn't scary or intimidating on the outside, and he wasn't sure that his insides were bad either.

Bram tried to think of an answer, to explain how he *was* bad, but the closer Master Mardybum came, the more flustered Bram grew. The teacher reached his desk and walked on with a sigh.

'It seems like killing people with

silence is your talent, Bram. Not the best power I've seen.' He frowned and turned his attention to his next victim. 'You, witch girl, tell me your worst tale. You look like you have a nemesis or two.'

The elf-witch, Mona, rolled her eyes upwards towards the

'GO AWAY'

badge on the top of her hat. She had rich brown skin and long dark hair that flowed down past her waist and there was an air of mystery about her. 'I do.'

'And who are they?'

'None of your business. You'll have to work that out for yourself.'

Master Mardybum's
eyes glowed red. 'Thinking
like a villain already and
not revealing your secrets
– I'm impressed. That kind
of thinking will win you
Villain of the Week.'

The teacher swished around
the room, gesturing to
pictures of himself on the
walls. He stopped to admire
himself in a full-length
mirror for a moment before
pointing to a large, ornate
frame with a
plaque underneath
that said: VILLAIN
OF THE WEEK.

'Each week,
I'll choose the

VILLAIN OF
THE WEEK

baddest, evilest student and crown them Villain of the Week. I don't give out the title lightly, so you must prove yourself in order to win it. Consider it a little competition between yourselves. Speaking of which, I'm *thrilled* to announce that as the sun sets at the end of this week, you'll all be competing as teams in a Mystery Maze in the Wicked Woods. At the end of the task, I'll name the student who stood out the most from the winning team as Villain of the Week,' he said.

'Do we *have* to work in teams?' Mona moaned. 'I'd rather complete the maze by myself than with this . . . useless bunch.' Her eyes lingered on Bram.

'Yes,' snapped Master Mardybum. 'My decision is final. Consider this your first lesson – even villains need allies.'

Mona had already switched off and was faffing with a net by her side, which sparked as her fingers fiddled with it. Bram had overheard her bragging about the net in the corridor before class began. Apparently, it was her weapon of choice, gifted to her by her parents, and it was said to entrap anyone that crossed her path.

What would happen . . .

Bram made
a mental note to
stay at least one metre
away at all times.

Master Mardybum continued. 'Right,
time to split you into teams. There will
be two teams – A and B. You'll decide
on a team name between yourselves
and submit it to me tomorrow morning.
Once submitted, you will *not* be able
to change it. And if you don't choose a
team name, then I'll select one for you
. . . and it will include the word *bogies*.
Understood?'

The students grimaced, but the Tooth
Hairy licked her lips. At the back of the
room, Bryan let off another revolting fart
in his sleep.

Master Mardybum clicked his fingers and a flame appeared in mid-air. It twirled and swirled, growing slightly larger than intended with all the methane gas in the air, and then gracefully transformed into a small piece of paper. The class watched in amazement as the teacher unfolded the note and read out the name 'Mal' as the

first member of team A.

The flames continued to appear and burn, sorting the students into their teams. Mona was the first member of team B and was quickly joined by a ghost named Sheila Boo, a skeleton named Tony and Bryan the Lion, who refused to wake from his slumber. Mal was joined in team A by the Tooth

Hairy, Mr Toad and Spike the Crocodile, leaving Bram and a cat named Jeeves as the last to be chosen.

Bram began to think. Which was the lesser of two evils? Which team looked *nice*?

Neither, was the answer.

'And the last member of team A is . . . Jeeves!' Master Mardybum announced.

A loud cheer came from the group – so loud that nobody even heard Bram being announced as the last member of team B.

He walked over to his new team members with a shy smile and offered out his hand.

Mona shook her head. 'No, thank you. I hate you all.'

Bram withdrew his hand in embarrassment and scratched his head. He'd hoped that he'd make friends *and*

learn how to be bad at Villains Academy.
But so far, he'd been embarrassed by his
teacher, rejected by his classmates and,
worst of all, his nose hairs were burning
with the rancid smell in the air . . . and it
was only his first lesson! It seemed that
being bad was going to be a lot of hard
work.

CHAPTER 2
NONSENSE
AND
NIGHTMARES

Bram's day went from bad to disastrous. Master Mardybum had gone on to perform a demonstration in villainous cape-swishing, followed by a lecture on the history of capes, including the gruesome tale of a teacher named Miss Fortune, whose cape was sucked down into the toilet. She was stuck in the pipes of Villains Academy for three whole days.

Master Mardybum then made the students of Class Z show off their best cape-swishing skills, which led to Bram getting tangled up and flicked in the eye as everyone swished to impress the teacher.

In the end, Master Mardybum declared Bram the *worst* cape-swisher he had ever seen, which made him shrink as low as possible in his chair, wishing he could disappear for ever.

Bram's classes throughout the rest of the day didn't go much better.

He had History of Evil with Chief Crabbatus, where he couldn't remember *any* facts about *any* villains throughout the *entire* history of time. After lunch, Whiz Warmbottom, the teacher of Villainous Qualities, shot Bram with sparks of fury when he couldn't present a single villainous quality. He further disgraced himself in his Bad Language lesson when he politely told Professor Pluto that he preferred *not* to use bad words, resulting in her calling him a

'**Shubblemegump**',

at which the whole class gasped. Bryan the Lion had gently patted Bram's back and said even his parents refused to use that insult. But Bram didn't understand what it meant. He was more upset about not being set *extra* homework, unlike the rest of his class. If he wasn't bad enough for extra homework, then what was he bad enough for?

As the bell rang to signal the end of lessons and the start of dinnertime, Bram shot out into the corridor before Professor Pluto could call him any more names.

'You should call your team *looooosers*,' Mal jeered at Bram as he pushed past him.

'And you should change your name to Screw-head, you oddity,' Mona responded and attempted to whack him with her net. 'Why didn't you stand up for yourself?' She scowled at Bram. 'You need to find your courage before you're eaten alive.'

'Sorry,' Bram said quietly and shrugged.

'Sometimes it's easier not to respond to hate.'

'You call yourself a villain?' she muttered as she walked away.

No, actually, Bram thought sadly. *I'm no villain, but I wish I was.*

His classmates disappeared down the corridor towards the smell of food. Bram followed the crowd quietly, but his stomach growled loudly as he reached the doors of the food hall. Inside, the air was alive with the racket of conversation.

The room was ginormous and had a domed stained-glass ceiling. Tree branches grew through the air and warped into tables and seats for the students. The walls, just like the corridors of the school, were filled with framed portraits of previous head teachers.

Vintage weapons had been transformed into lights and hung from branches as if they were fireflies in the forest. At the far end of the room was the food counter, where an ostrich wearing a frilly pinafore hurried around serving the hungry villains.

As Bram shuffled through the food hall, he noticed Mal and his new teammates from Master Mardybum's class huddled round a table, talking excitedly. He was so distracted and nervous that he almost stood on a snail at the back of the food line.

'**Oi**, fur ball, watch where you're going! You almost trampled me to death,' the snail jeered.

Bram jumped. 'Sorry, I didn't see you there.'

'Well, next time I'll pierce you with my poisonous spikes, okay, shuzzbutt? What class are you from, anyway?'

'Class Z,' Bram mumbled in reply.

'Ah, fitting. Class ZOOPID. They always put the useless ones in Class Z, I heard.'

Bram dipped his head and his heart sank. Was that true? Had he been put in the class for terrible villains? There were only five classes in each year group (V, W, X, Y and Z), meaning that only about fifty lucky wannabe-villains were accepted into the school every year to prove they had what it took to become the villains of the future.

Behind them, a deep voice rumbled. 'Can you get a move on? We can't all afford to move at your pace, and I'd like to eat something this century, if possible.'

It was
Bryan.

'You looking for a fight?' the snail threatened.

In hanger (hunger and anger), Bryan swiped at the snail and sent it rolling through the food hall beneath the tables. Bram waited a moment before rejoining the queue.

Villains Academy was a school for baddies all right – was *everyone* going to be this mean and rude?

The queue moved slowly. Even slower than the snail. When Bram finally reached the front of the line, the ostrich threatened to peck him to death if he didn't hurry up and choose something to eat. So he settled on a sour potato with blood beans and made his way round the hall to find somewhere to eat it.

'You can't sit there. Now . . .

MOOOOVE!'

An overly fluffy monster snapped at Bram as he attempted to sit on the seat opposite.

'Okay, sorry,' Bram muttered as he scuttled off the seat quicker than you could say 'bumbershins'. Feeling very out of place, he wandered along the rows of tables, looking for somewhere else to sit.

'Hey, fluffy. You can sit with me,' a voice called out. Bryan the Lion was sitting at a table by himself, eating bright-green spaghetti off a stupendously large plate.

Bram thought about the snail that Bryan had swatted like a fly earlier and hesitated. Bryan seemed like a loose cannon.

'I don't bite,' Bryan said with his mouth full. 'Not unless you annoy me.'

Bram shrugged and sat down. What's the worst that could happen? It might be good to make friends with a fierce lion anyway. Plus, they were teammates now. 'Thanks,' he mumbled.

'You're very shy, aren't you?' Bryan asked. 'That's not a bad thing, as long as you *can* be bad. Are you bad?'

'I can be bad. It's . . . it's just first-day nerves,' Bram lied. He wasn't about to tell the truth to angry-pants over here.

'Good. Well, fill your stomach, enjoy your dinner and meet me upstairs in ten. We've got a team name to sort out, scarewolf.'

The sun disappeared over the horizon and Bram felt satisfyingly full as he sat in the dormitory he was sharing with his new teammates. Well, everyone apart from Mona, who refused to share a room with anyone and stayed stubbornly in her campervan on the grounds of Villains Academy. The other classes had been

split up into teams too, though apparently Master Mardybum was the *worst* form tutor they could have been given. Plus, they also had him for lessons that he specialized in, like Poisons and Physical Escape.

'What about the Phantom Hunters?' Sheila the ghost cooed to her teammates, making herself as long as possible. Her body was transparent and flexible, allowing her to glide through tight spots. Plus, she was freezing cold to touch. She was dead, after all.

Bryan yawned and rolled his eyes. 'No.'

'The Fantasticals!

Or the Sonny Peeps?

Or the Tasty Toes?'

Sheila continued.

'No, Sheila. What about you, skeleton? Any ideas for team names?'

The skeleton shrugged his shoulders. 'My name's Tony. Full name: Skele-tony Le Bone. But you can call me Tony. What about something like the Golden Gang?'

Sheila wiggled her tail. 'I love that, bony Tony! Though, I'm not golden. What about the Transparent Sheilas?'

'We're not all called Sheila, Sheila,' Bryan grumbled. 'Bram . . . anything?'

'What do we all have in common?'
Bram replied, wracking his brain.

'I like **huffle**pops, 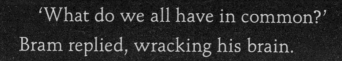'

cakesicles,

flibberts,

and CHOCOLATE!

Not cheese, though. That stuff gives me
nightmares,' Sheila said.

'Mmmm, cheese.' Bryan drooled.

'Food is okay.' Skele-tony shrugged.

'It goes straight through me.'

Bram laughed. 'Okay, so food is a common interest. That, and us trying to be villains. Maybe we need something incorporating the two?'

Bryan yawned . . . again. 'It's been a long day and the sky has gone dark, meaning the world is telling us to sleep. So why don't we sleep on it?'

'You've slept a lot today, sonny peep.' Sheila bounced around. 'You should get that checked out.'

'I'll check you out of Villains Academy if you don't be quiet.'

'Okay,' Bram interjected, trying to distract Bryan. 'We can share our ideas with Mona in the morning. It's a team decision, after all.' But by the time the last word exited Bram's lips, Bryan was already fast asleep.

No matter how hard he tried, Bram couldn't get to sleep.

Bryan farted *a lot*. Tony's bones creaked and he liked to sleep *sitting up*, which convinced Bram that he was plotting to kill them all. At one point in the night, he even took off his head and left it on his pillow whilst his body went for a wee. Sheila zoomed about the room, stretching herself into all sorts of shapes and talking to herself.

Bram's thoughts haunted him with the possibility of failure and being kicked out of Villains Academy. He felt so flustered that he eventually gave up trying to sleep and sat on the windowsill with a book to distract himself.

The school stood in a
clearing in the middle of
the Wicked Woods.
Moonlight shone
on the tips

of the trees, strange howls
echoed in the darkness and
an ominous mist clung to
the ground. Two lakes sat
beside each other, said to
be filled with menacing
monsters and a tunnel that
led directly to the centre

of the earth. Gravestones grew out of the
grass around the lakes and Bram shivered
at the thought of the dead that might
come to haunt him from beneath.

A blazing light from the campervan on
the grass below caught his attention.
A figure in a large hat slammed the door
of the campervan shut and skulked across

the grounds. Bram wondered what Mona was doing out so late, but his mind soon darted back to Master Mardybum's team name request. He had lots of ideas, but scrapped every single one at the thought of embarrassing himself in front of his classmates.

Eventually, he climbed back into bed because his toes had started to develop frostbite, but just as he was at last falling into the land of nod, a loud cockerel screamed outside, telling them all to

WAKE UP!!!

With a deep sigh, Bram forced his eyes open and thought about the day ahead. He was tired, cold and surrounded by the most disturbing room-mates. But today was a new day and he was determined to make sure it was better than yesterday.

He rubbed his bleary eyes, let out a yawn and thought about a cup of something nice and warm. And then he remembered that just as he had drifted off to sleep, he'd finally thought of a good team name to share with the rest of the group.

Today he was going to *kill* it.

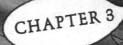

CHAPTER 3

FURYFLUMPS

The morning air was cool and a dense
mist hung closely to the ground. Class
Z had filled their bellies at breakfast
and were now waiting outside the
greenhouse for their first lesson on
mixing poisons, with none other than
Master Mardybum himself.

Mona adjusted the **GO AWAY** badge
on her hat. 'So, what team names have
you come up with?' she asked, looking

fresh from a night of peace and quiet in her campervan.

Bram took a deep breath. This was his moment. 'The Cereal Killers,' he said proudly. 'It combines two of our common interests – food and being villains. Plus, it's punny.'

'It's stupid,' she replied.

Bram's shoulders collapsed in defeat. He'd spent most of his restless night conjuring it up and he'd really thought she was going to like it.

'Well, have *you* thought of any names, Mona?' Bryan yawned. 'Ugh, it's so early.'

'No. Anyway, I don't want to be in this team.'

'But you have to be in our team!' Sheila said. 'If you don't like the Cereal Killers, we have more names. There's the Transparent Shei—'

'No, we vetoed those,' Tony butted in, removing his hand and shoving it in her mouth. *Literally.*

At that exact moment, Master Mardybum appeared and ushered them into the greenhouse. 'Settle down! Settle down!' his voice echoed. 'It's an exciting day, I know. But there are some *very* dangerous plants in this greenhouse. I want *no* funny business – and *no* touching. I won't be responsible for clearing up your bodies. Understood?'

Naturally, the students began looking around and poking at the plants. Apart from Bram, who moved as far away from them as possible. Especially from one in the corner of the greenhouse that twisted and snapped when anyone even breathed near it.

'Now, time for your team names! I hope you've all managed to agree on one? Your teams are very important. They're an integral part of Villains Academy history. Even *I* still meet up with my old villainous teammates, the Soul Sisters, from time to time.' Master Mardybum remained blank-faced and Bram tried not to laugh. The teacher continued, 'I wanted us to be called the Soul Destroyers,

but I was out-voted. Anyway,
Mona, why don't you kick us off?
What will your team's name be?'

'The Cereal Killers,' she replied
confidently, completely stealing Bram's
idea. Bram's mouth dropped wide
open, and his heart sank to the tips
of his furry toes.

'Interesting. How did you come up with that?' Master Mardybum asked.

'Well, we discussed our common interests, which are food and being villains. The Cereal Killers combined them both.'

'*Ingenious!* Well done, Mona and team.'

Bram wished he had the courage to speak up and say something, but instead he stayed silent and gave Mona his best death stare . . . not that she noticed.

The opposing team sniggered at them. 'What a *stupid* name,' Mal whispered.

'And what's your team name, Mal?' Master Mardybum asked.

'The Overlords.'

Master Mardybum considered this for a moment, before patting Mal on the shoulder with a proud look on his face. 'Fantastic! One of the best team names

I've heard in years.'

Mal stuck his tongue out behind Master Mardybum's back, which infuriated Mona so much that she flicked a bogie at him.

'Now that's sorted, please return to your stations and begin today's task – to make a sleeping poison. You'll find all the instructions on your worksheet. Please don't bother me with any of your questions,' Master Mardybum said and relaxed back into a rocking chair, sipping a mug of steaming green tea.

The instructions for the sleeping poison were complex. Bram didn't know what the majority of the ingredients on the worksheet were, and none of the instructions – to squish, pulp, pummel and bash them – made any sense either. Luckily, Mona was an expert at making poison . . . even if she was reluctant to admit that she was part of their team.

She squished moonberries and bashed cucoma leaves in silence, whilst Sheila attempted to quiz her about her life. Tony tried to help her by cutting open the shell of a frostbite with his scythe, but it flew straight across the room. The snapping shrub in the corner leapt to catch it, mistaking it for prey, and wobbled dangerously, before toppling to the ground at Master Mardybum's feet.

'AAAAARRRGHHHHHHHHHH! YOU IMBECILE!'

Master Mardybum jumped as the shrub tried to bite his ankles. He ran over to a nearby pot of silk-pea, pulled the plant out of the soil and began whacking the shrub with the silk-pea roots. (Master Mardybum had previously told the class that similar plants like bindweed hated silk, which made silk-peas extremely useful for defence.) As he moved towards the corner of the greenhouse, a piece of broken glass *crunched* beneath his foot.

Where the snapping shrub had once stood, fragments of glass were strewn all over the floor and the window pane beside it was shattered, as if someone had broken in the night before. Scattered on the ground amongst the glass were some of the leaves of the shrub.

'The Furyflumps,' Master Mardybum whispered, his eyes growing wide with worry.

'WHO HAS TAKEN THE FURYFLUMPS?'

he suddenly shouted.

The class stared at him, bewildered. Bram's anxiety rose inside him.

'I am not joking. *Who* has stolen the Furyflumps?' Master Mardybum shook with anger as his eyes darted around the room. 'The green fruits of the snapping shrub! They've all gone – and they were definitely here yesterday!'

'It could have been anyone!' Mona spoke up. 'There are hundreds of students at Villains Academy.'

'Furyflumps are *very* rare and *very* expensive. They're *rumoured* to make people angrier . . . badder, if you wish. And there's only one person here that I can think of that desperately needs to be badder. Isn't there . . . Bram?'

Bram felt like he was about to puke all over Master Mardybum's robes. 'No . . . I-I-I—'

'You, you, you what?' Master
Mardybum mocked.

'I didn't steal anything. I was with my
team all night; they can vouch for me!'
Bram pleaded.

Master Mardybum raised an eyebrow
and turned to Bram's classmates. 'Can you?'

Bryan shook his head.
'I fell asleep.'

'As did I,'
Tony replied.

'Me too,'
said Sheila.

'And you, Mona?' the teacher asked.
'I was in my campervan all evening.
Don't ask me,' Mona said.

'But you saw me! You all saw me!'
Bram cried. He began to shake in distress.
Why had his teammates betrayed him
when they knew full well that he was in
the dormitory with them all night? He
wanted to defend himself, but his voice
choked up, leaving him with nothing to
do but stand there in disbelief.

Master Mardybum towered over him
and his eyes burned into Bram's soul.
'You've done nothing but disappoint me
since you arrived, werewolf. You will
never receive Villain of the Week. Sadly
I don't have enough evidence to prove that
you stole the Furyflumps, so I can't expel
you on the spot, but consider this your
first strike. Two more and you're out.'

Bram's mind whirred with the
possibility of being kicked out of Villains
Academy and shaming his family . . .

and on his second day. He hadn't even done anything to deserve the strike – apart from *not* stealing the Furyflumps.

He had never been a bad person and struggled to feel angry, even on a full moon. His parents sent him to Villains Academy hoping that being surrounded by *bad* people would turn him bad too. But so far, it had only made him quieter, if that was possible.

All he wanted was to make his parents proud and graduate Villains Academy as a true villain. His parents were famous villains back home in Wolfden. They were always causing chaos – terrorizing the farmers, having LOUD parties on a full moon and frightening the local sheep to death. His dad's favourite anecdote was about the time he scared a family of sheep so badly that they shed their wool right there in the street and ran away in terror . . . naked to the bone. His other dad knitted jumpers for Bram's whole family out of the wool.

They were true villains, specializing in everything and anything *bad*. People, animals and fellow villains – even *heroes* – travelled across the land to enlist their expertise for bad deeds and services of terror.

If Bram had to return back home with anything *but* official villain status, he'd be a laughing stock.

'I'm sorry, Master Mardybum. I—' Bram began, trying to salvage the situation.

'I don't want to hear your excuses. I'm going to have to report this theft to Governor Goodlethorn,' Master Mardybum replied. 'And I've decided that I'm going to give everyone detention tonight, for being so wonderfully bad. But you will *not* serve detention with the rest of your classmates, Bram, because you're not *bad* enough to deserve it.'

Bram held back the tears that threatened to burst from his eyes. First no extra homework, and now no detention. He was well and truly messing up his villain education. He spent the rest of the class in silence with his head bowed, silent tears trickling down his fur.

But it seemed that not everyone was as bad as they appeared. When Master Mardybum wasn't watching, Tony slipped Bram a tissue from his pocket, Bryan gave him a gentle pat on the back and even Sheila *tried* to give him a hug – but instead flew straight through his head, giving him brain freeze.

It was only Mona that refused to comfort Bram. Instead, she focused on completing the poisonous sleep draught

in record time, much to the delight
of Master Mardybum. Bram made a
mental note to memorize the recipe and
to hopefully, one day, impress Master
Mardybum himself.

CHAPTER 4

MASTER MARDYBUM'S OFFICE

The second day at Villains Academy passed just as slowly as the first, and the lack of sleep weighed heavily on Bram's eyelids.

He had come to the conclusion that his teachers were true villains . . . and the students were just as bad. In Deadly Injuries, when Bram accidentally caused a fatal wound to *heal* by enthusiastically patching it up, Matron Bones had told

him that he couldn't kill a person if he
tried. In Astrology, Guru Gertrude taught
them how to read the stars to stay one
step ahead of their enemies. In one of
her trances, she said that the stars had
aligned against Bram and predicted him a
horribly *boring* death.

In the afternoon, Class Z's final lesson of the day was on how to master the *death stare* with Master Mardybum. Bram dreaded entering the classroom and felt even worse when the teacher challenged them to have a stare-off and timed them to see who performed best.

Bryan fell asleep after one minute. Mona lasted one minute and eight seconds. Mal came just behind her with one minute and two seconds . . . and Tony stood there for over five minutes before Master Mardybum declared time up. (It helped that Tony's lack of eyelids meant it was impossible for him to blink.)

When it was Bram's turn, his eyes began to water after ten seconds. Then Mal made a loud *bang* that caused him jump . . . and he blinked. Master Mardybum was so angry with Bram that he made him sit with his eyes closed for the rest of the lesson.

Luckily for Bram, the Cereal Killers were more than happy to keep him up to date on the latest happenings in the classroom. Sheila whispered that Master Mardybum's eyeballs had rolled out of his head because they'd become so dry from not blinking. Tony said that Spike the Crocodile had eaten Master Mardybum's long, billowing sleeves. And Bryan explained that he gave the teacher a piggyback ride around the room for extra demerits, causing them all to double over in quiet laughter.

Bram beamed at the bonkers images in his mind and thought about how he could befriend Mona, who was the only one who had stayed silent.

ZIIIIIιιNNNGG! The bell rang,

announcing the end of the day.

'Right, class. See you later at detention. Apart from you, Bram,' Master Mardybum said with a smirk.

Bram responded with a gloomy nod.

'Did I tell you to open your eyes?' Master Mardybum said in a threatening tone.

'How am I supposed to see where I'm going?' Bram asked, shutting them as he attempted to leave his desk.

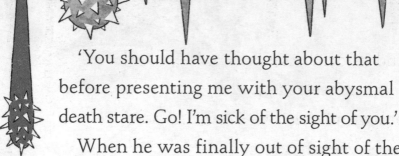

'You should have thought about that before presenting me with your abysmal death stare. Go! I'm sick of the sight of you.'

When he was finally out of sight of the teacher, Bram opened his eyes and a new idea had taken shape in his mind. He *was* bad enough to deserve detention and he was willing to do whatever it took to prove Master Mardybum wrong. It was time to break into detention.

Master Mardybum's office was up on the top floor of the teachers' tower at Villains Academy, away from the classrooms

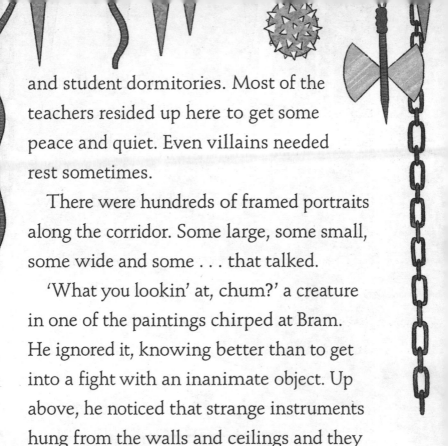

and student dormitories. Most of the teachers resided up here to get some peace and quiet. Even villains needed rest sometimes.

There were hundreds of framed portraits along the corridor. Some large, some small, some wide and some . . . that talked.

'What you lookin' at, chum?' a creature in one of the paintings chirped at Bram. He ignored it, knowing better than to get into a fight with an inanimate object. Up above, he noticed that strange instruments hung from the walls and ceilings and they looked suspiciously like weapons . . .

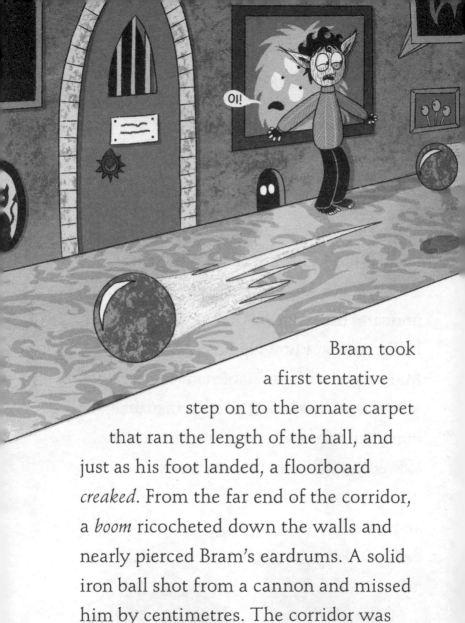

Bram took
a first tentative
step on to the ornate carpet
that ran the length of the hall, and
just as his foot landed, a floorboard
creaked. From the far end of the corridor,
a *boom* ricocheted down the walls and
nearly pierced Bram's eardrums. A solid
iron ball shot from a cannon and missed
him by centimetres. The corridor was
booby-trapped.

'What *is* this place?'
Bram whispered to himself.

'You shouldn't be here, Sonny Jim,'
a furry-headed man from another
portrait threatened.

'Do you know where Master
Mardybum's office is?' Bram asked.

'Sure. It's behind that door. Why don't
you take a look?'

Bram glanced at the handle of the
door. Spikes jutted out from every angle
and a low, worrying rumble came from
behind. 'Erm, no, thank you. I think I'll
just find it myself.'

He set off down the corridor as fast as
his feet could carry him. He stumbled into

a suit of armour and accidentally triggered three more booby traps. An axe fell from the ceiling, slicing the knight's head clean off. A net dropped down, encasing the armour, and twirled away like a tornado. Finally, a small door opened by the skirting board and a family of angry cleaner mice flooded the corridor, yelling at him for making a mess, and began whacking his ankles.

The smallest mouse, feisty and with long whiskers, chucked a pair of frilly underpants at his head in annoyance.

Bram attempted to escape as quickly as he could, but the pants on his head covered his eyes. He tripped over cannonballs, rogue legs of armour and possibly even a mouse or two. With a hard thump he landed on the floor and shuffled away from the squealing mice like a constipated slug, removing the underwear as he went.

There were more doors and frames down this end of the corridor. Most had plaques with names on them. Bram shuffled discreetly along with his back against the wall, being careful not to be seen or heard by any of the occupants. In the distance, the irritating jeers of Mal echoed from behind a door that was labelled

MASTER MARDYBUM

on the shiniest sign he had ever seen.

'Gotcha!' Bram whispered with relief. Before he began to doubt himself, he pushed on the handle and started to walk forward.

But it was locked.

His nose squished into the door in a painful splat. He twisted and turned the knob, but no matter how hard he tried, it would not open. He banged on every surface, attempting to alert his classmates and teacher, but nobody came.

With a huff of frustration, Bram dropped to the floor and began shouting under the door. 'OPEN THIS DOOR . . .

NOW! OR ELSE!'

Still nothing.

So he took matters into his own hands. Beside the entrance to Master Mardybum's office, Bram had spotted a small door that was used by the cleaner mice. On his hands and knees, he began to squeeze himself through the door and into the tiny tunnel. His bottom scraped the ceiling and he moved quickly, trying not to think about getting stuck.

Bram felt a prickle of excitement. A prickle of . . . badness? He was going to prove to everyone that he was a villain. He continued shuffling like a worm, moving his body through dust and cobwebs, until eventually a sliver of light appeared at the far end.

In a burst of energy, Bram erupted into
Master Mardybum's office . . . but only
his front half emerged.
His bottom was
STUCK!
His classmates immediately turned
to the noise.

'HIS BIG
BUM'S STUCK!'

'No, I'm not,' Bram insisted, his fur burning hot.

'He is!' Spike the Crocodile laughed.

Master Mardybum had tears streaming down his face. 'Stop it! Please, stop it! That's the funniest thing I've seen in years. Is this your attempt to get into detention?'

Bram nodded, and frantically tried to free his bottom as a wave of embarrassment washed over him.

'Well, I'm afraid detention is over,' Master Mardybum announced, much to the confusion of the class.

'But it's only just started!' Mal insisted.

'Can't have too much of a bad thing. Not when there's *good* people about.' He gave Bram an evil look as he sat down at his desk.

One by one, his classmates left the office in fits of laughter. The Cereal

Killers shrugged and smiled at him
awkwardly, too afraid to interfere with
Master Mardybum watching over them.

'Excuse me, sir?' Bram asked bravely.

'Oh. You're still here?' Master
Mardybum looked up from his desk with
a bored expression on his face.

'Can you help me?'

Master Mardybum sighed and clicked
his fingers. In an instant, Bram felt
little pairs of hands pushing against his
bottom and he was propelled out of the

tunnel like a cork from a bottle.

'Now that the mice have done your job for you, you can get out of here,' Master Mardybum said.

'Thank you,' Bram muttered on his way out.

'DON'T USE YOUR MANNERS AT ME!'

Mardybum roared as the door closed behind him.

Bram dashed down the corridor of talking picture frames that screamed at him. At the top of the stairs, he flung himself round the banister and slid all the way down in a hurry.

At the bottom, he crashed into (and through) a screeching Sheila, who had come zooming out of the library. The remnants of something sticky and green

were splattered around her mouth, which made him cringe in disgust as it sprayed him. She wailed about having terrible wind and how she urgently needed the loo, but didn't stop to apologize to Bram for the brain freeze, or the goo that had ruined his woolly jumper.

What the devil has got into her? Bram wondered.

Chapter 5

HIDE-AND-SHRIEK

The cockerel screamed, 'WAKE UP!!!'

Despite the loud awakening, Bram lay comfortably in bed like a warm burrito all wrapped up in his covers, thankful to have finally had some restful sleep.

'READY FOR A NEW DAY, CEREAL KILLERS?' Sheila shrieked.

'I swear, if you don't lower the decibels I'll eat you,' Bryan grumbled.

'Terribly sorry, sonny peep. I'm just *so*

excited for a new day. I think you'd have trouble eating me, though. I'd go straight through you. Plus, I'm already dead!'

'Tony, shove your hand in her mouth again,' Bryan said.

Tony tore off his leg and threw it at Sheila. It propelled straight through her head and then shattered against the wall above Bram's head. Bones scattered around the room and the pinky toe landed in Bram's hair.

'Wow, what a head rush!' Sheila whooped, clearly thrilled to have a foot thrown at her.

'I think this is yours,' Bram said, holding out the pinky to Tony.

'Ah, thanks, mate. I'm always losing that,' he replied.

'Will you all *please* be quiet?' Bryan complained, throwing his paws over his head.

'Come on, sleepyhead, get up! **BIG DAY! LOTS OF FUN TO BE HAD!**' Sheila yelled.

Bryan leapt from the bed with the energy of a kitten. He swiped at Sheila in the air, who twirled away from his grasp as if they were playing a game of cat and . . . ghost. But the excitement quickly got too much and Bryan ended up letting out a reeking fart, which made everyone, even Bryan, charge out of the room.

'What have we got this morning?' Tony asked as they made their way to the food hall. The walls of the corridors were plastered with posters to warn students that visits to the greenhouse were strictly prohibited after hours. Bram was sure they hadn't been there yesterday and thought about his run-in with Master Mardybum during Poisons. He hoped that all of this wasn't because of him, even though he'd done nothing wrong.

DO **NOT** ENTER THE GREENHOUSE

OR ELSE...

'Physical Escape,' Sheila answered Tony's question. 'I wonder what we'll do. Oooh, I do hope it's frightening people. That's my favourite.'

Over his breakfast of bread rolls and bloodfruit, Bram thought about what physical activity he would be escaping from in today's lesson. The anxiety rose inside him as he imagined a roaring beast chasing him, or being held captive by Master Mardybum. But he pushed the feeling back down, determined not to let it get the better of him.

Beside him, Tony scoffed a pile of squishy green fruit.

'Those look tasty! I didn't see them on the counter.' Bram smiled and leant over to take one of the fruits from his plate.

Tony screamed in alarm and inhaled all the fruit down his windpipe in one

big mouthful, before whacking Bram with his arm, which he had removed from its socket.

'Sorry,' Bram apologized, batting him away. 'Noted that you don't like to share food.'

Bryan peered at him out of the corner of his eye as he gobbled up a mountain of bloodfruit that stained his muzzle with scarlet juice. When he had finished,

he sauntered over to the water fountain in the middle of the food hall and multiple villains shrieked in horror at the bloodstained beast. He guzzled litres of water, causing the fountain to turn into a bloodbath, and then he let out a brash

BURP.

'Okay, *now* we can start the day, Sheila,' he said, winking at her.

Class Z stood in the Wicked Woods, waiting for Master Mardybum to arrive.

The Overlords had already begun with their taunting.

'Can you even run, Tony?' asked Jeeves the Cat. 'Or do your bones fall apart?'

'Yes, I can run. Plus, I can remove my bones and use them as weapons,' Tony replied with a swish of his cape, flashing the white bones underneath.

'Cool!' said Spike the Crocodile.

'Spike,' Mal butted in. 'They're our rivals, so stop being nice. You won't get anywhere as a villain with that attitude.'

Tony was just about to remove his arm and whack Mal with it when Master Mardybum glided into the clearing.

'Wonderful day to be in the Wicked Woods,' he said, waving his sleeves dramatically and flashing a frown at Bram. 'Today we have a physical *activity*.'

'Is it *frightening people*? Please say it's frightening people,' Sheila hollered.

'No, Sheila.' Master Mardybum rolled his eyes. 'Today we will be playing a game of HIDE-AND-SHRIEK!'

The students groaned.

'Now, now. It's essential for you to learn the art of evasion. The best villains know how not to get caught. You'll work in your teams. There are two piles of dragon eggs by the tree over there, and each pile is a different colour – though don't worry, they're not real dragon eggs. As if a formidable dragon, one of the ancestors of evil, would let you take its eggs! You'd be burnt to a crisp before you even got near its nest. Half of the eggs have been filled with gold glitter and the other half with blue gunk. Both teams are hiding and seeking. If you see a member of the opposite team, splatter

them with one of your eggs, which will show me who's been found. If you're still clean by the end of the game, I'll know that you have the skills to evade capture when you're a *proper* villain. The cleanest team at the end will be declared the winners. Overlords, you take the glitter eggs. Cereal Killers, you take the blue gunk eggs. Happy hide-and-shrieking! Oh, and just to note, stay inside the boundary that I've set – we don't want to be attracting the real dragons now, do we?' Master Mardybum winked wickedly before retiring to a tree stump to read a book about knitting.

Bram was suddenly both terrified and thrilled at the thought of bumping into a real-life dragon, and his fur began to tingle with excitement.

W<small>EEE</small>E<small>EEE</small>W<small>EEEEEEE</small>W<small>EEEEEEE</small>!
went the siren, announcing the
start of the game.

The Cereal Killers gathered
together in the shadows of the
Wicked Woods.

'We need to split up. We'll be harder
to find separately,' Mona whispered,
before adding, 'and DON'T get
caught, Bram.'

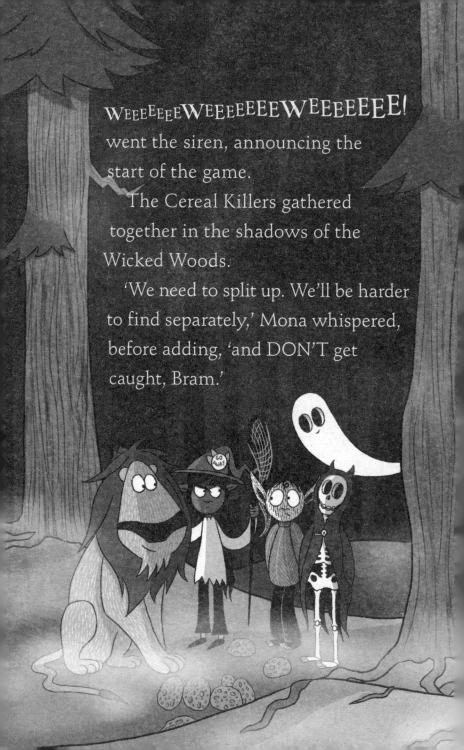

'Why *me*?' Bram defended himself. 'What about Tony and his creaking bones, or Bryan, the *massive* lion . . . ?'

'Be *quiet*,' Mona snapped. 'If I see one sprinkle of glitter on you then you're dead meat. You know that stuff doesn't wash out. On second thoughts, Bram, you'd better stay with me so that I can make sure you don't mess this up for us.'

'Byeeeeeeee. Have fun, sonny peeps!' Sheila cooed as she floated into the treetops.

Bryan bounded away and Tony had already disappeared.

Mona shoved a handful of blue dragon eggs into Bram's arms.

'I can't carry all of these!' he protested.

'Shove them in your pockets, then, nitwit,' Mona replied, hiding eggs under her hat.

The forest was silent. Bram and Mona crept between bushes and tree trunks.

SPLAT!

'AHHHHHHHHHH!' came a scream from nearby. 'Not the eyes!' Bram saw a flash of glitter, followed immediately by the Tooth Hairy chasing a sparkly Sheila through the forest.

'Brilliant. Ten seconds in and Sheila's already got herself caught.' Mona frowned.

'It's not all about winning, you know, Mona.'

'It might not matter to you, *Bram*. But Villain of the Week will look great on my record when I graduate Villains Academy and take over the world.

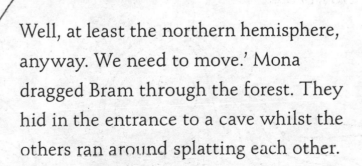

Well, at least the northern hemisphere, anyway. We need to move.' Mona dragged Bram through the forest. They hid in the entrance to a cave whilst the others ran around splatting each other.

The Tooth Hairy was soaked head to toe in blue gunk as Sheila flung eggs down on her from above. Spike was having a battle with Bryan, who looked as if he was falling asleep. Jeeves watched from a branch above, ignoring everyone, and Mr Toad was attempting to *eat* Tony.

Bram felt a horrible urge to laugh at the chaos but Mona shoved an egg into his mouth. Mal had just wandered right into

their path. He looked around suspiciously before beckoning down Jeeves. 'Are we still on for tonight?' Mal whispered.

'Of course. Once Master Mardybum is asleep we'll gather at the greenhouse.'

The greenhouse? Bram thought. Why would the Overlords be gathering at the greenhouse? The whole school has been warned not to visit after hours since the Furyflumps incident yesterday. Unless . . . that's exactly why they're going there tonight?

'I think they're going to steal the Furyflumps,' Bram whispered to Mona, the pieces of the puzzle falling into place.

She elbowed him in the ribs. 'Shut up and listen, will you!'

'Okay, spread the word to the others. And whatever you do, don't let the Cereal Killers find out,' Mal said, looking over his shoulder to check nobody was around.

'Noted,' Jeeves agreed, before climbing back up the tree.

The back of Mal's head made Bram seethe. He readied his arm to throw an egg at him when Mona stopped him. 'No. He'll know we were here,' she whispered. 'This way, we can catch the Overlords at their own game. I have a plan.'

'Why do I not like the sound of this?' Bram moaned.

'Because you're a chicken dressed as a werewolf.'

SPLIT! SPLAT! SPLOSH!

Bram was hit in the face three times with glittery eggs that exploded all over the pair.

'That was your fault for being so loud.' Mona glared at him before smashing one of her own blue eggs on the top of his head.

Chapter 6

SABOTAGE

After losing the game of hide-and-shriek the Cereal Killers walked back to their dormitory, covered in glitter and gunk. Bram felt a familiar pang of guilt in his stomach for letting the team down. Especially because he was the person covered in the most glitter. The other Cereal Killers insisted that they didn't mind; in fact, it was the most fun they'd had at Villains Academy so far. All except

Mona, who skulked off to her campervan, refusing to talk to any of them.

'She'll come round eventually,' Sheila said as she shook her body like a glittery raincloud.

Tony took off his head and tipped it upside down, the glitter pouring out like a waterfall. 'Yeah, it'll be fine. She's just a hard nut to crack.'

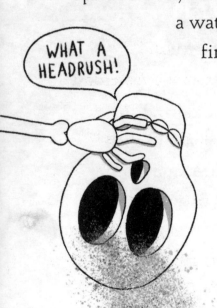

WHAT A HEADRUSH!

'I thought we were bonding,' Bram mumbled, thinking back to them hiding in the cave together. 'We overheard something when we were hiding today. We think the

Overlords are up to no good. Mona said she had a plan, like she wanted us to work together.' Bram really did want to work with her and prove that he wasn't a scaredy-wolf.

'What did you hear?' Tony asked.

'Something about visiting the greenhouse. Maybe it's to do with those stolen Flumpyflumps that Master Mardybum was so upset about yesterday,' Bram replied.

'*Furyflumps?*' Bryan asked, his eyes widening in alarm.

'Oh, sonny peep! We can't let them!' Sheila insisted uneasily.

Tony nodded furiously in agreement. 'Yeah, we can't let them.'

Bram was taken aback by the sudden distress and determination of his teammates. But, at the same time, a warm feeling filled him up inside. None of them had dismissed him like Mona had – they believed in him.

'What was Mona's plan, then, sugarplum?' Sheila asked.

'I don't know. But it didn't sound *good*,' Bram replied.

A wicked grin spread across all three of the Cereal Killers' faces.

'My favourite kind of plan.' Bryan beamed.

'STOP!' a fierce-looking mouse squeaked as the gang reached the main door to Villains Academy. 'If I see *one drop* of glitter

on these floors, I will personally stuff
your pillows with Guru Gertrude's nail
clippings,' it threatened.

The Cereal Killers looked at each other
in bewilderment.

'That sounds *LOVELY*!' Sheila replied
and floated straight through him, then
began shimmying herself along the
wooden floors of Villains Academy,
leaving a trail of glitter behind her like a
snail.

Bram wished that he could have just one
ounce of the confidence that Sheila had.

The rest of the day was relatively quiet,
which Bram was thankful for. Over
dinner, he rushed down his backlebeet
soup and headed straight to the
dormitory, hoping for five minutes of

peace. But just as he began to rest his head on his pillow, a light breeze tickled the fur on his cheek and his eyes snapped open to see Mona mere centimetres away.

'DON'T HURT ME!' Bram shouted in fright.

Mona cackled wickedly, dodging Bram's flailing arms. 'You're such a wimp.'

'You shouldn't sneak up on people like that,' Bram said, angry at being woken from his wolfnap.

In the corner, Sheila laughed her tail off and mocked, *'Don't hurt me.'*

'The sun is only just setting and the evening is about to begin. Why were you even asleep?' Mona asked.

'Because *some* of us haven't had enough sleep since arriving,' Bram replied.

'Well, wakey-wakey, because we have a plan to make,' Mona declared.

Sheila floated over and pushed her eager eyes between the pair. 'What are we doing? When are we doing it? And, most importantly, can I get some snacks on the way?'

'We're going to ambush the Overlords,' Mona said, grinning, as the rest of the Cereal Killers returned from dinner.

'Has this got something to do with the conversation you and Bram overheard earlier?' Bryan perked up.

'Yes,' said Mona. 'The Overlords are planning to meet by the greenhouse tonight. And I think we can all guess why. I say we tip off Master Mardybum and ambush them.'

The gang looked at Bram expectantly. He knew this was going to end badly, but at the same time, his body filled with adrenaline and excitement at the thought of doing something he shouldn't. It felt good to be *bad*. 'Okay,' Bram said.

'I'm in,' Tony replied.

'Ah, why not. I could do with a walk.' Bryan stretched his legs.

'So, what about these snacks?' Sheila
asked.

As the sky settled into evening, Bram
found himself in the treeline of Villains
Academy with the other Cereal Killers,
waiting for the Overlords to arrive.

Mona had slipped a note under Master
Mardybum's office door, tipping him
off about a great heist that was going to
happen at the greenhouse. All they had
to do now was wait.

They waited . . . and waited. Bram
crouched down low. But nobody arrived.

Stars pierced the sky as their
surroundings descended into darkness.
Owls hooted in the distance and other
scarier-sounding animals growled deep
in the Wicked Woods. Bryan farted . . .

a lot, and even Tony joined in with the odd toot. Sheila didn't stop talking, and slowly, the light from Villains Academy grew faint as time passed by.

'Maybe you heard wrong?' Tony said, picking his pelvis up off the floor with a creak.

'Shush,' Mona snapped. 'We definitely heard right. Unless they know we're on to them.'

'Let's just go back,' Bram said, his

excitement well and truly gone.

'Always giving up,' Mona muttered.

Bram ignored her comment and pushed himself up off the floor. He didn't want to stay out all night on a wild goose chase. 'I think we're wasting our time. I'm heading back.'

'Don't you dare go with him, Tony. I'll happily come over there and pull off your legs,' Mona threatened as Tony attempted to leave. So he stayed put.

As did Sheila and Bryan, who had fallen asleep together in the bushes.

'Yes, why don't you go?' Tony encouraged.

'Night, then.' Bram shrugged and began walking across the grounds towards Villains Academy, feeling slightly sad that nothing had happened and worried that he might miss out on the action by leaving now.

Up ahead, a tall, thin silhouette loomed in the middle of the grass. Bram mistook it for a statue, until it let out a small cough and a smooth voice flowed through the air. 'Well, well, *well* . . .'

Master Mardybum stood in the moonlight staring wickedly at Bram, who was now inconveniently standing just metres away from the greenhouse.

'M-Master M-Mardybum,' Bram

stuttered, wracking his brain for an explanation. 'Lovely evening for a walk.'

In the dark, Master Mardybum's eyes began to burn red. 'Don't even pretend that's why you're out here. Even you, an imbecile with no brain, will have seen the warnings to stay away from the greenhouse after hours. Consider this your second strike. One more and I'll personally make sure you leave Villains Academy for good. Do I make myself clear?' Every word that came out of his mouth was slow and piercing.

Bram's insides churned with annoyance at how unlucky he had been to leave the treeline at that exact moment. It definitely didn't help that Master Mardybum clearly had a grudge against him for no reason whatsoever. 'Yes, sir. But—'

'And I don't see why you're so keen

to get your hands on the Furyflumps anyway. I didn't say they *do* make you badder. I only said they were *rumoured* to. This is a lesson in paying attention, Bram. It's a myth that they make you angry. All they actually do is give you terrible wind. Now don't let me see you near this greenhouse again.' He flicked his fingers and shot a spark of anger up into the sky like an exploding firework.

Bram nodded anxiously and scuttled across the grass as quickly as his feet could carry him.

In the distance, he heard Mona's campervan door slam shut as she escaped Master Mardybum's wrath. Ahead of him, he spotted Sheila, Bryan and Tony creeping into the school with what looked like a pile of fruit in their arms. The same kind of fruit that Tony had been eating at breakfast the other day. Bram was both confused and enraged. It had been their idea to come here tonight, and it was Mona's plan to outsmart the Overlords. But all it had done was get him into trouble. And not the good kind, either.

And to make matters worse, the Overlords were pressed up against the glass of a latticed window upstairs in Villains Academy. Sneers and laughter were painted across their faces.

Bram's heart sank.

How did they know he would be out

in the grounds at this time? Why did they look so pleased with themselves?

Then it hit him. They knew he would be out here because they had orchestrated the whole thing to trick the Cereal Killers. It hadn't been a coincidence that the Overlords were talking loudly about their plans . . . The Cereal Killers had been set up.

Chapter 7

SQUABBLE

Bram stomped through the halls of Villains Academy, filled with rage. He was on his final strike, all because he had been accused of stealing a silly green fruit that *apparently* made you bad – though, according to Master Mardybum, even that was a myth. But he had never been near a Furyflump in his life!

The only squishy green stuff he had seen was whatever had been splattered around

Sheila's mouth yesterday. It was *still* stuck to his jumper.

Bram stopped on the stairs for a moment.

That was a lie. He *had* seen a green fruit at breakfast this morning, and Tony had seemed very protective of it.

Bram continued up the stairs, but with each step he took, the cogs in his mind whirred faster. It couldn't be a coincidence that the Cereal Killers were having a fruity midnight snack this very minute. Bram's telling-off had created the perfect distraction to break into the back of the greenhouse . . . But it couldn't be true. His friends wouldn't do that, would they?

And just like that, everything clicked into place.

Bram reached the dormitory and

Brain
juice

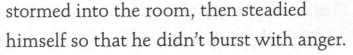

stormed into the room, then steadied
himself so that he didn't burst with anger.

'Oh, Bram, you're alive. Thank
goodness! I thought Master Mardybum
might have fried you,' Sheila squealed
and rushed over to inspect him.

'Alive and better than ever,' Bram said
sarcastically. 'Are you all here? I have
something I want to say.'

'Mona isn't here. She's in her
campervan,' Tony replied.

Bryan yawned. 'Can it wait until the
morning? I'm really tired.'

'No. It can't. Now sit up and listen to
me!' Bram said firmly. His heart was
thumping – he couldn't remember ever
feeling this upset before.

'Oh, sonny peep, he's angry,' Sheila
muttered and began hiding herself under
her bedsheets.

Bryan growled. 'Go on.'

Even Tony stopped flossing green goo from his teeth to listen.

'I'm still really angry that you all let me take the blame back by the greenhouse. But right now, I have bigger fish to fry . . . I know what you've been up to,' Bram said with determination.

The gang looked at him, confused. 'What?' they said in unison.

Bram gathered his courage. 'You've *all* been stealing the Furyflumps, haven't you?'

Sheila gasped aloud at the accusation.

Tony dropped his head.

Bryan sat up straight. *'Excuse me?'*

Bram squared his shoulders. 'You've been stealing Furyflumps and letting me take the blame. You think I'm stupid, but I've seen you. *All* of you.'

Sheila turned paler than a ghost, if that was possible.

Bryan's face filled with rage. 'How *dare* you accuse us of stealing Furyflumps! Believe it or not, *we* don't need them like you do. We can be bad by ourselves.'

Bram's heart beat a little faster. Maybe he had made a mistake? Maybe they hadn't stolen the Furyflumps and he'd just got the wrong end of the stick? And here he was, accusing the only people who had tried to be friends with him since he'd arrived at Villains Academy.

'But you've been farting . . . a lot,' he mumbled to Bryan.

'Is that your only evidence?' Bryan roared with laughter.

'No, it isn't,' Bram continued. 'Just now when Master Mardybum caught me, he told me the only thing Furyflumps are good for is giving you wind. And you fart a LOT, Bryan. Then, Sheila, you were farting *loads* the other day when you came out of the library – and you had something sticky around your mouth that you splattered me with. Plus, Tony was eating that squishy green fruit at breakfast the other morning. I bet that's why you wouldn't let me have any.'

'You should be ashamed of yourself for even *thinking* that about us,' Tony replied, clearly hurt.

'But surely it all points to one thing,' Bram said, trying to make sense of everything. 'How do you explain the pile of fruit you were just carrying across the grounds?'

'Those weren't Furyflumps!' said Bryan. 'They were the dragon eggs from hide-and-shriek. We dumped them in the Overlords' dormitory on our way in as payback. And if we were stealing Furyflumps, we wouldn't be stupid enough to do it when Master Mardybum was so close. You're determined to accuse everyone, aren't you?'

'Well, sonny peep,' Sheila added. 'We don't need you accusing us. We don't want people like that in our team.'

'Agreed,' Bryan added, and Tony nodded, causing his head to fall off again.

Bram felt tears welling in his eyes and he struggled to think of what to say in response. He didn't have much evidence, so he couldn't be one hundred per cent certain that it *was* them who had been stealing the Furyflumps.

But what about Mona? He'd seen her skulking across the grounds on the very first night and there was no logical way to explain her evening stroll. 'Well, I think Mona has definitely been stealing them! I saw her out in the grounds on our first night.'

'Of course you did. Why don't you go and ask her, then?' Bryan replied with an eye-roll. 'You can get her vote on whether she wants you in the group whilst you're there too.'

Those last words stung – and Bram knew exactly what Mona's answer would be. The group stared at him expectantly.

'Okay, I WILL!' Bram shouted, and stomped out of the dormitory.

Bram marched back across the grounds of Villains Academy and towards Mona's campervan. He was beyond upset at the way his team had spoken to him. And to make it even worse, the Cereal Killers were watching him from the dormitory window above.

The campervan loomed up ahead. The bland green surface and windows shone like a spark of light in a black hole. Bram hammered on the door.

'Mona! It's me – Bram. Open up.'

Mona did not answer.

'MONAAAAAAA!'

Bram howled.

The door burst open and bounced off the side of the campervan with a loud *crash*. 'What on *earth* are you doing?' Mona snapped. 'Do you know what time it is? I am *this* close to zapping you into the next century.' She flicked her fingers angrily at Bram and tiny sparks of magic shot out.

Bram balled up his fists. 'We need to talk.'

'We can talk tomorrow,' Mona said and attempted to shut the door. But Bram blocked it with his body and pushed it wide open.

'No, we're going to talk now,' Bram insisted, feeling his courage rising.

'What's wrong with you? Why are you so angry?' she asked, frowning.

'Well, firstly, you just *left* me at the greenhouse. It was *your* idea to go and ambush the Overlords. But I was the one who got into trouble for it. I'm on my second strike because of that. One more and I'm gone. Have you even figured out yet that the Overlords

set us up? We walked right into their trap.' Bram paused to take a breath before continuing. 'You've been treating me – all of us – like you're better than us since we arrived, and I'm fed up of it. You're not too bad or too villainous to be my friend, you're just a . . . just a

SHUBBLEMEGUMP!'

Bram spat out the last word, still not knowing what Professor Pluto had meant when she used it.

Mona stepped back at the insult and narrowed her eyes with menace. 'I don't know what you're talking abou—'

Bram pushed on. 'You all let me take the blame in Poisons and be the scapegoat for your Furyflump theft. You all leave me when anything goes wrong – in detention when I got my bum stuck, and again just now at the greenhouse.'

Mona smirked, trying to contain a laugh.

'STOP LAUGHING! Nobody ever takes me seriously and I've had enough of it.'

Mona raised her eyebrows. 'And what are you going to do about it?'

GO AWAY

The anger inside Bram was bubbling like a cauldron and he knew there was only one way to make his team listen to him. 'From now on, *I'm* going to be the team leader of the Cereal Killers, and it'll be *me* that makes the decisions.'

Mona rolled her eyes. 'We're all doomed, then.'

Bram's resolve weakened. 'Why do you say that? I'd be a good leader!'

'You're a terrible villain, Bram, and I don't want to be in a team with someone like that, let alone be led by them.'

Bram clenched his fists tighter. 'So you don't want to be in our team?'

'I don't want *you* in our team,' Mona replied.

That was four votes for kicking him out of the group. Mona's words stung, but Bram wasn't about to let her know that.

'Fine. I guess that's our friendship over.'

'We were never friends in the first place. I didn't come here to make friends,' Mona said flatly.

The second blow cut through Bram like a knife. 'You're just scared to open up to people. You think you're above being friends with anyone, but that just makes you a loner,' Bram snapped.

Mona's face turned bright red. 'I am *not* a loner. I just don't want to work with pathetic little villains like *you*.'

Bram took a step away from Mona, his whole body slumping. Was she that ashamed of working with him?

'Now go away,' Mona added.

Bram summoned the last bit of courage he had left and let rip. 'Enjoy your sad, lonely life in your campervan, then!'

As the last words left his mouth, he

started to run back across the grounds,
knowing that he had pushed it too far.
His feet pounded over the grass, as Mona
shot sparks of magic at him through
the darkness. The magic was angry
and chaotic, bursting around Bram in
eruptions of emotion.

'YOU BEST RUN FASTER, BRAM!'

Mona screeched from her doorway. Tears streamed down her face and the jets of magic were as blue and cold as her heart. Stealing a glance at the window above,

Bram noticed that the lights were off and the Cereal Killers were no longer watching.

He had fallen out with his only friends at Villains Academy and the truth was just sinking in. He was totally alone.

Chapter 8

KEEP YOUR ENEMIES CLOSE...

Bram woke up feeling worse than ever. Memories of last night replayed in his mind and he dreaded getting out of bed and starting the day. Everyone had turned against him; even his own teammates were now his enemies.

When Bram arrived at Master Mardybum's classroom for his first lesson, Class Z were already in their seats, waiting patiently with smirks on their faces.

'Oh, look who it is,' Mal jibed.

Bram hung his head in shame. He couldn't look anyone in the eye.

'Now, now, villains. Please, sit your bums down and play nicely,' Master Mardybum said as he arrived with a swish.

Bram felt a shiver shoot down his spine at the sound of the teacher's voice and he rushed to his seat before he could be shouted at for being too slow.

'Ewww!' Sheila shouted. She was jiggling up and down on her chair, but her tail was stuck to it. She whirled around the air in panic, whacking Jeeves on the head and screeching something about gum.

Behind her, Bryan leapt up and hopped around the classroom grabbing his bottom.

Tony stood up with a clattering of bones as his pelvis remained stuck to the seat, and the realization suddenly hit Bram. *Oh no.* His seat was sticky too and his fur was clinging to it.

Master Mardybum looked on at the chaos in confusion. 'What's going on?'

The Overlords chuckled to themselves. It was Mal who let out the first booming laugh.

At the front, Mona rolled her eyes and ignored the frenzy, but stayed firmly on her seat.

Maybe she truly was working alone now after their argument last night? But Bram was pretty sure that she had gum on her chair too. The thought soon disappeared when an out-of-control Tony began battling the Tooth Hairy – Tony using his arm and the Tooth Hairy using her deadly hair, which wrapped itself around his body.

'STOP!' Master Mardybum roared, causing everyone to shudder into silence. 'Enough of this nonsense. You will not fight amongst yourselves whilst I'm here. I can't be dealing with the hassle. Sit down, all of you.'

Tony slotted his arm back on to his body and reattached himself to his pelvis.

'Now, Overlords, I must say, I'm rather impressed with you. Great pranking, well done! Cereal Killers, you could take some notes.' Master Mardybum winked.

Sheila cast an annoyed glance at Bram.

What now? thought Bram. He wasn't the one who had put gum on their chairs.

'Actually, that was a very fitting prank for the start of today's lesson, because

I'm going to be speaking to you about keeping your enemies close,' Master Mardybum continued. 'Do any of you have enemies yet?'

Mal's hand shot up, as did Mona's.

'Doctor Jenkells,' Mal said proudly. 'He's the evil doctor that gave me these scars.' He gestured to the stitches on his face.

Master Mardybum nodded in approval. 'Excellent. What about you, Mona?'

'I had a run-in with Mother Nature once,' she said.

The class gasped.

'Splendid work!' Master Mardybum replied. 'It seems the rest of you need to up your game. When I was a young villain, I had *many* enemies. Most of them were superheroes that weren't a match for me, but my *biggest* enemy was Dust Danger.'

'So it *is* true that you destroyed Dust Danger?' Jeeves asked.

Master Mardybum smiled, clearly pleased at the attention. 'Dust Danger was one of my closest friends. I met her here at Villains Academy and we were the best of pals. We completed many evil missions together and destroyed more heroes than I can count or remember. But I don't want any of you making the same mistake as I did. I let Dust get too close. I trusted her too much – so much so that I never saw the signs. You need allies and friends as a villain, just as much as any hero, but you must always have your own back. Dust Danger didn't have mine.'

'What happened, sir?' Spike asked.

'She betrayed me. Whilst we were on a mission, I learnt that she was working undercover and had switched over to the *good* side. She was double-bluffing me in order to take me down. So I destroyed her before she had the chance to destroy me. Remember, have your own back, and never be too afraid to destroy your friends. Keep your friends close, but your enemies closer.'

The Cereal Killers cast looks at each other and Bram felt the hairs prickle on the back of his neck. They wouldn't think twice about destroying him now.

Mal gasped in delight, Spike gave a loud *whoop* and the Tooth Hairy clapped her hands in delight. But whilst most of the students found Master Mardybum's act truly admirable, Bram felt sickened by it. Dust Danger was his friend and he had destroyed her. Gingerly, Bram raised his hand.

'Yes, Bram?' Master Mardybum asked, annoyance tingeing his voice. The whole class stared at him in surprise.

'I'm confused.' Sniggers filled the air, but Bram continued anyway. 'The other day, you taught us that even villains need allies . . . yet now you're saying not to trust anyone. Which one is it?'

'I'm telling you to have allies,' replied the teacher, 'but be on the lookout for any signs that they're turning *good*. Never be afraid to call out a friend and destroy them if you need to.'

Bram nodded,

but secretly thought Master Mardybum
was spouting nonsense. How could
he live his whole life never trusting
anyone? He needed people around him
that *truly* had his back. He swallowed
the lump that had suddenly formed in
his throat. He was starting to see why
the Cereal Killers had kicked him out
of their group. He hadn't trusted them
and had accused them of a theft they
didn't commit. No wonder they weren't
talking to him.

'Speaking of which . . .' Master
Mardybum went on, 'I'm pleased to see
that some of you aren't getting on. But
my opinion hasn't changed since our
very first lesson, so for those of you that
have requested to work alone . . . or kick
a certain person out of your group, the
answer is no.'

'You can't be serious?' Mona protested.

'Oh, I am *VERY* serious,'

Master Mardybum replied.

'Being a villain is hard work and you can't give up at the first hurdle,' he continued. 'From now on, I expect to see you working as a group, or I'll give you *merits*. Understood?'

'Yes, sir,' Mona muttered.

Bram shuddered at the thought of receiving merits and stayed quiet. Those were the last things he needed when he already had two strikes on his record.

'Now, let's crack on with the rest of the lesson. There's lots to teach you before the Mystery Maze tomorrow. Oh, it's going to be a *terrible* day,' he said, laughing wickedly.

Chapter 9

STARGAZING

The rest of the day was semi-disastrous, but fairly quiet compared to the start of Bram's week.

The Overlords had ruined everyone's lunch by adding hot sauce to the food and making it inedible. Bryan was so upset that he burst into tears in the middle of the food hall, and Sheila and Tony had to take him away because he was terrifying everyone. Even Mona reluctantly helped by casting a spell to make him weightless. Bram watched from a table in the corner by himself and Mona stuck out her tongue at him as they left the room.

In the Art of Craftiness lesson that afternoon, their teacher, the Mouldy Knight, was impressed with the abstract painting Bram had created from splattered blood, which made Bram beam with pride. It felt nice to be praised for a change.

In the evening, the Cereal Killers and the Overlords settled on the grass outside Villains Academy in silence whilst Guru Gertrude taught them about the stars. She fixed herself into some sort of trance whilst staring at the North Star, muttering something about wanting to rule the whole universe.

Bryan let out a long fart. Then another,
and *another*.

'Ugh, Bryan. Why do you fart so
much?' Mona complained.

The group looked at each other
awkwardly. Tony shoved his hand in
Sheila's mouth before she could say a

word and Bryan started licking his feet.

'What?' Mona frowned. 'Am I missing some inside joke?'

'No,' Bryan replied, growing bashful. 'I have a dairy intolerance, but I can't resist cheese. I just love it so much, even though I know it gives me wind. I've got a secret stash under my bed.'

Bram began awkwardly plucking the grass from the ground beneath him to avoid eye contact with the group. Bryan's dairy intolerance explained why he had been farting a lot recently, and it made Bram feel even more ashamed for accusing him of stealing Furyflumps.

Beside them, Guru Gertrude, who had been fixated on a spot in the sky, began twitching. 'The universe is not happy, my villains,' she said. 'There is a misalignment in the stars that has been caused by the extreme levels of tension amongst you all. A grudge cannot be held for ever and arguments must be forgotten. If you do not start working as a team again, then I fear the worst.'

Mona rolled her eyes. 'What a load of rubbish.'

'The stars do not lie, dear child,' Guru Gertrude warned her. 'And true villains do not ignore the truth. You would be wise to remember that.' And with a huff, Guru Gertrude walked over to where the Overlords were sitting, presumably to explain what the universe had in store for them.

The Cereal Killers glanced at each other awkwardly as they sat in silence.

'Maybe Guru Gertrude is right,' Tony spoke up. 'Maybe we should put everything that has happened behind us.' He took off his arm and held his hand out to Bram. 'Can you do that?'

Bram smiled. He wanted nothing more than to be friends with the Cereal Killers again. The guilt of accusing them had preyed on his mind non-stop since last night, and he didn't want to spend his

time at Villains Academy without them
by his side. He took Tony's hand and
shook it. 'I can. And I'm sorry.'

'We're sorry too,' Sheila said and
launched herself at Bram to give him a hug.

'All forgotten,' said Bryan, swishing
his tail in delight.

The group looked at Mona
expectantly. But she didn't say a word.

Instead, she looked back at them blankly. Bram wondered whether that was her way of apologizing, or if she still hated his guts.

'She'll come round,' Sheila whispered. 'We have to work as a team from now on or the stars will fall from the sky and burn us to death.'

Bram laughed. 'I don't think that's *quite* what Guru Gertrude meant.'

'Oh, it is!' Tony agreed with Sheila. 'She also said that I can have your puddings for the rest of the term too.'

'Okay, now you're being ridiculous.' Bram chuckled.

'That's no way to talk to your teammates,' Bryan replied. 'You have to share your puddings with ALL of us, or we'll be doomed for the rest of eternity!'

Chapter 10

A TOUCH OF CHEATING

Over pudding, the Cereal Killers
discussed plans for the Mystery Maze.
None of them had a clue what to expect,
but Mona remained suspiciously quiet.
It was only when the team had given
up trying to guess what the maze might
have in store for them that they noticed
she had disappeared.

'Where did Mona go?' Tony asked.

'Oh, devils. The stars are going to start

falling any minute,' Sheila wailed.

'We'll be fine,' Bryan assured. 'In fact, look! There she is.' Mona strolled towards them through the food hall and sat back down without a concern in the world.

'Well . . . ?' Sheila asked. 'Where have you been?'

Mona grinned. 'I was sorting out our plan.'

'What plan?' Bram asked.

'You'd all better get your act together because we've got about half an hour until Master Mardybum falls asleep. I just slipped him a little sleeping poison to help. The plan is to break into his office and steal his plans for the maze.'

The Cereal Killers grinned in awe, but Bram frowned. 'You're going to *cheat*?'

'Yes, *we're* going to cheat. Have you

got a problem with that, Bram?' Mona shot back.

'No,' Bryan stepped in, trying to defuse another argument between the pair. 'What Bram meant to say was that all good villains cheat and it's a brilliant idea. Isn't that right, Bram?'

Desperate to be a good villain, Bram swallowed the words on the tip of his tongue 'Erm . . . yep,' he squeaked.

'Great.' Mona smiled. 'Let's go.'

The Cereal Killers crept through the halls of Villains Academy as the rest of the students returned to their dormitories, hoping to use the busyness of the corridors and cover of nightfall as the perfect opportunity to sneak into Master Mardybum's office.

Bram pushed down the prickling feeling of anxiety growing in his chest at the thought of everything that could go wrong . . . and the thought of taking the blame once again.

As Bram had discovered earlier in the week on his way to detention, the corridor in the teachers' tower was filled with booby traps. A spiked wrecking ball swung up and down the centre of the passageway, nearly knocking Bryan off his feet. Sheila thought she was clever and better than everyone else by

flying through the air and not touching
any of the walls or ceiling . . . only to
be covered in heaps of slime that shot
out of cannons at the far end. Even Tony
managed to hobble on like a trooper
when his foot got stuck in a clamp
halfway up the corridor.

When they eventually reached Master
Mardybum's door, it was only Bram and
Mona that were left unscathed.

'Let's be quick and quiet. Get in, get
out. No dilly-dallying, okay?' Mona
ordered.

The team rushed into Master Mardybum's office one after another. Mona ran straight over to the teacher's desk and began rifling through the drawers. Tony scoured the far corner and turned house plants upside down. Sheila checked up high, pressing bricks in the walls for any secret compartments. Bram searched high and low, looking for hidden clues. And Bryan stood on lookout with his ear pressed to the door that led through to Master Mardybum's private quarters.

'hello'

'Anything?' Mona whispered as she emptied out the final drawer.

'Nothing,' Bram replied.

'Me neither,' Sheila said.

'Is a tea strainer any good?' Tony asked, holding up a small instrument in the shape of a skull.

'Maybe he's going to drown us with tea in the Mystery Maze?'

SO TIRED

'Oh, don't be stupid, Tony. When are you going to use that brain of yours?' Sheila replied.

'He doesn't have a brain, Sheila,' Bryan said, laughing.

'I *do*,' Tony protested.

'Ha! No, you don't!' Sheila giggled. 'BRAINLESS!'

Tony ground his teeth furiously. 'Come say that to my face.'

'You don't have a face, JUST A SKULL!' Sheila roared. Tears of laughter slid down her cheeks.

Tony launched the tea strainer with all his strength across the room and *through* Sheila. She screamed and rolled around on the floor melodramatically. Mona tried to wrestle an iron paperweight out of Tony's hand as he advanced on Sheila, and Bram looked around anxiously, worried about

all the noise they were making.

'What the devil is going on here?' Master Mardybum's voice boomed out suddenly, and his shadowy figure appeared. He looked around at the pandemonium. 'And *what* are you doing in my office?'

Mona's sleeping poison must have worn off. The Cereal Killers looked to Bryan, wondering why he hadn't warned them, but the answer was clear. Bryan had fallen asleep.

'*Well*?' Master Mardybum roared.

Bram caught Sheila's gaze as she struggled to contain a smirk, which made him burst out laughing.

Master Mardybum's eyes burned. 'What is so funny? Have you got anything to say for yourself, Bram?'

'No. It's just . . .' He glanced down at the teacher's flowery night robes, trying – and failing – to suppress a grin, even though his heart pounded with nerves at the thought of riling up his teacher. 'Nothing.'

Master Mardybum's cheeks burned as bright as his eyes. 'I bet you all think you're

so clever, don't you? Coming in here to steal the plans for the Mystery Maze. But surely you can't be stupid enough to think I'd leave them lying around?'

The Cereal Killers looked at each other in embarrassment.

Master Mardybum continued. 'Nice try. But there's no way to cheat. I'm not surprised to see you here, though, Bram. You've been caught in the act too many times now. You're the most pathetic excuse for a villain that I've ever met in my entire life.'

Bram's eyes began to sting. He refused to cry in front of Master Mardybum – and in front of his teammates.

'Consider this a strike for all of you, for your pathetic attempt at theft. Now, I'd call that three strikes, wouldn't you, Bram?' Master Mardybum's words hung in the air.

Bram's heart dropped. Three strikes and he was out. That's what Master Mardybum had said before. Now he had to return home and leave Villains Academy for good. He had ruined his chances of proving to his dads that he could be a true villain and the shame would live with him for ever.

Sheila did a little sob and threw herself around him. Even Bryan and Tony joined in the group hug.

'No.'

Mona's voice rang out, loud and clear.

Bram turned to her in confusion.

'It wasn't Bram's fault,' Mona said. 'It was my idea to come here and steal the plans. If anyone deserves to be punished, it's me.'

Bram stared at her in disbelief. Had she really just taken the blame for him? He'd thought she still hated him, but she'd put her neck on the line to save his skin.

Master Mardybum considered her words. 'If you're telling the truth, then you're an imbecile. If you're covering for your little friend over there, well, let's just say I thought you were wiser than that.'

Mona hung her head, the brim of her hat hiding her face.

'Bram, today must be your lucky day. Don't pack your bags *just yet*. But you can  all get out of my office immediately. And *never* break in here again, or you'll be gone quicker than you can say Villains Academy. Understood?'

'Yes, sir,' they said in unison and exited the office as quickly as they could.

'Lovely pyjamas by the way, sir.
Where did you get them from?' Sheila
asked as she flew through the door.

Master Mardybum glowed with anger.
'I won't think twice about destroying you
if you mention this to anyone. Now, you

have three seconds to get out of here.'

A fireball of fury followed
the Cereal Killers down
the corridor as they ran for
their lives, with whoops of
laughter trailing in their wake.

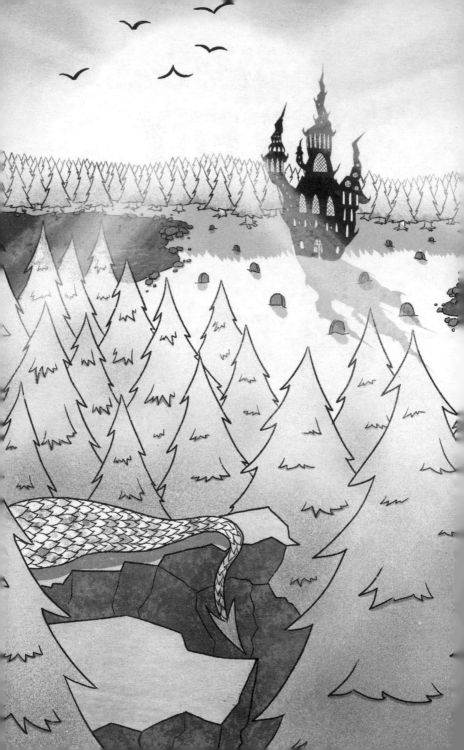

Chapter 11
THE MYSTERY MAZE

The rising sun streamed across the grounds of Villains Academy. The early birds caught the worms and pecked them to death in the glimmering rays. Bram leapt out of bed with a new lease of life because he was finally making real friends at school. After the drama of last night, even Mona had joined them in their dormitory, which made him feel like they'd finally turned a corner.

And even more excitingly, today was
the day of the Mystery Maze!

Classes were cancelled and they had
a whole day of planning ahead of them.
Bryan snored loudly, Sheila twirled
through the air, Tony was reattaching his
head and Mona had already left in silence.

'MOOoOOooOOOORNING!'

Sheila yelled.

'Are you nervous? I'm nervous,' Tony
said.

'Pooping myself,' Bram agreed.

'Terrified,' Sheila joined in. 'I bet
Master Mardybum has some more
devilish tricks up his sleeve after last
night.'

'Let's not think about that just yet,' Bram replied. 'Shall we get some breakfast?'

'DID SOMEBODY SAY BREAKFAST?'

Bryan bounded up and was the first out of the door.

The Cereal Killers spent the day huddled together in Mona's campervan, preparing for the Mystery Maze. They quizzed each other on everything they'd learnt so far, tried to predict what Master Mardybum was planning and even had pretend battles between themselves. Though Mona took it a little too seriously and ended up offending Sheila when she grabbed her tail.

Slowly, the shadows outside grew longer as the sun dipped behind the trees of the Wicked Woods, and the sky settled into a calming shade of purple. The Cereal Killers gave up studying and turned to more important matters – playing exploding snap.

'We should get going. The last thing we need is to be late,' Bram announced as he attempted to pack away the box of exploding snap cards that burst around him, making Bryan fart in fright.

The gang began to disperse from the campervan quickly to get away from the smell. Tony was so revolted that he began posting his bones through the moon window to escape quicker and Bram threw himself out of the door.

'Will you all just calm down?' Mona insisted as Sheila flew through the wall. 'We've got a Mystery Maze to win.'

'Yes, Mum,' Sheila agreed with a salute.

B4D

Mona shot her a deadly look. 'I mean it.'

In the distance, the Overlords stood
by the main door of Villains Academy,
whispering to each other. As the Cereal
Killers approached, they fell silent and
crossed their arms with smirks on their
faces. 'Ready to be beaten?' Mal taunted.
'That Villain of the Week title is ours.'

'Sure thing, meat-head,' Mona replied.

The door behind them creaked open and the looming shadow of Master Mardybum glided out from within. 'Excellent – you're all here. Come on, then, let's see what you're made of,' he sneered. The class followed him towards the Wicked Woods, and with every step, Bram felt like he might wet himself from fear.

They walked for what felt like an eternity until they stumbled into a clearing illuminated by moonlight. Towering ahead of them were walls of thick shrubs that pierced the air. They were three metres high and wobbled in the evening breeze, making the maze seem like a living, breathing creature. And when the entrance began to growl, Bram was certain that they were going to be eaten alive before the night was out.

'Now, time for the rules. You win once every member of your team is out,' Master Mardybum said. 'I have the final say. *No* arguments.

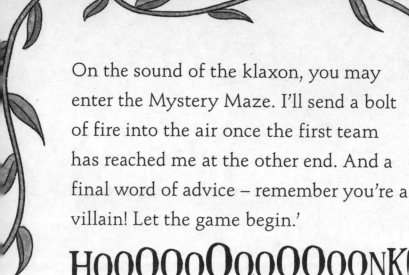

On the sound of the klaxon, you may enter the Mystery Maze. I'll send a bolt of fire into the air once the first team has reached me at the other end. And a final word of advice – remember you're a villain! Let the game begin.'

HOOOOOOOOOOOOOONK!

The Overlords barrelled into the maze ahead of the Cereal Killers. Hedges grew out of the ground with gnarled roots that twisted and turned in all directions, weaving a labyrinth of paths. Some routes led to dead ends, where terrifying monsters jumped out with no warning. Mona led the pack, but the deeper they got, the harder the maze became to navigate.

'We need to stay together!' Mona shouted to her team. She gripped Bram's hand and dragged him along, fearful that they might lose each other.

As they turned a corner, an enormous troll hammered the ground like a game of whack-a-mole and Mona shoved the gang back the way they had come. 'Nope. Not that way.'

Around another corner, vampires lurked and threatened to suck their blood when the gang got too close. Mona screamed at one to **'BOG OFF, BOG BREATH'** which made the vampire . . . cry. In unison, the Cereal Killers began insulting the vampires, thinking of the WORST and MEANEST things they could say.

Even Bram managed to call one a
'**SHUBBLEMEGUMP**',
which made the vampire run away wailing.
Professor Pluto would have been proud.

In one section, wild bindweed vines
shot out of the shrubbery and tried to
drag the group away. Tony quickly lost
a limb, and Bryan was grabbed at from
all angles. Bram dropped to the floor and
began to crawl quickly, his heart
hammering in his chest, but his
paws slipped on a silky weed
that sprouted out of the ground.

What is this? Bram wondered. But as he looked closer, he noticed that it wasn't a weed at all. It was a silk-pea – the plant that Master Mardybum had used to deter the snapping shrub in the greenhouse. Sheets of silk grew from their roots and they were everywhere! 'SILK-PEAS!' he bellowed. 'EVERYONE PULL THEM UP!'

The Cereal Killers looked at him in confusion. In that exact moment, Mona was tackled by a furious vine and toppled to the floor. Bram yanked a long sheet of silk-pea out of the ground and began frantically swishing it like a cape, remembering everything Master Mardybum had taught him.

The sharp corners of the silk flicked at the vines, making them recoil. Bram danced his way over to Mona, flicking and swishing, spinning and slapping.

'Remember what Master Mardybum said – bindweed hates silk!' he said as he pulled Mona free. 'Now grab a silk-pea, use it as a cape and whip those vines away!'

For the first time all week, Mona listened to him. She pulled up a silk-pea and began desperately

flicking and **swishing**

it like a cape. Within moments, everyone was free, and they left the bindweed far behind to

SWISH SWISH BISH

enter the next stage of the maze.

'That was genius, Bram!' Bryan commended him. 'Thank you for saving us.'

Bram smiled. 'No problem. You'd have done the same for me.'

The group looked at each other guiltily. Bryan nodded gingerly.

Bram laughed. 'Okay, maybe you wouldn't have done the same for me, but that's why you're all better villains. Let's just keep going.'

'No,' Tony protested. 'I can't do this any more.'

'Pull yourself together, bony Tony!' Sheila insisted.

'No, he's right, Sheila,' Bryan agreed. 'We're not better villains than Bram. In fact, we're rubbish villains! I'm sorry, Bram. You were right,' Bryan said, his voice wobbling.

'Right about what?' Bram asked, suddenly forgetting that they were in the middle of a dangerous maze.

Tony hung his head.

'We *have* been stealing Furyflumps.'

'Sheila, Tony and I have been stealing them. And they've done nothing but give us terrible wind,' Bryan said.

Bram's mind spun. He had been right all along . . . and they let him take the blame! *Plus*, they'd lied to him when he confronted them. 'But . . . but why?' was all he could manage to mutter.

'We don't feel like villains. We don't have the urge inside us to be bad,' Tony replied. 'Bryan has never managed to roar, Sheila has never frightened anyone to death like she says she has, and I can't bring myself to kill anyone like I'm supposed to – my dad is the Grim Reaper. We're so sorry, Bram. We never wanted to lie to you or make you upset. I hope you can forgive us.'

As Tony's words sank in, Bram let the

anger that had been bubbling up inside him wash away. 'I didn't realize you all felt that way,' Bram replied softly. After everything that had happened this week, he never expected to hear that his friends felt exactly the same as he did. Maybe he wasn't so alone after all. 'Do you feel the same way too, Mona?'

Mona cast her eyes to the floor to avoid looking at the group. 'Deep down I don't feel like a true villain either, but I've never stolen Furyflumps to make me bad. I thought I could prove my badness

by winning Villain of the Week all by
myself. That way my parents would be
proud. My mum always taught me that
a good villain works alone, but I can
see now that she was wrong. I'm better
for having all of you around me and I'm
sorry for being so mean. Oh, and, Bram,
I'm sorry for stealing the credit for our
team name. I love the Cereal Killers.'

Sheila's eyes glistened with pearlescent
tears. 'That was beautiful. But don't
worry, it's not just you. We're all terrible
villains,' she said.

'Agreed,' Tony chimed in.

'I'M A TERRIBLE VILLAIN!'

Bryan shouted at the top of his lungs.

Bram grinned, which then turned into
laughter as everyone began to shout. It
was the type of hysterical laughter that

comes from deep within, because if you don't laugh, you'll fall apart. The sort that only happens between friends.

'I'M A TERRIBLE VILLAIN!' he joined in.

'I'M A TERRIBLE VILLAIN!' Mona screeched.

Bryan placed his paw in the middle of everyone and gave them a smile. One by one, without having to say anything, they all placed their paws, hands, tails and bones on top of each other and huddled together as a group.

'THE CEREAL KILLERS!' they yelled in unison.

'Right, team, we've got this. Let's go!' Mona announced as they ventured further into the maze together.

They followed the path through a
flowering archway made of iron. Sheila
whispered that she was **POOPINGLY
PETRIFIED** and Mona held out her
net in defence. Slowly, they edged their
way into an open clearing. There was a
moment of relief that there was no troll
raring to bludgeon them to death or vines
ready to grab them, then Tony squealed.

From behind the fountain, in the
centre of the clearing, a band of Wood
Elves emerged with nets in their hands,
ogling at them in delight.

'Stay calm,' Mona whispered. 'Don't blink and they won't hurt you.'

Bram's heart began to pound out of his chest. He was *terrible* at death stares. He had only lasted ten seconds with Master Mardybum!

But it was too late, Bryan had already blinked, and the Wood Elves shot around them like darts. They moved faster than lightning, and before Bram knew what was going on, the world had turned to bedlam.

CHARGE!

In one swift swoop, an elf gathered Tony up in its net and swung him round like a toy. Sheila dived into the air to avoid them, and Bryan laughed as four of them leapt on to his back because they tickled.

'We need to get away from them! Protect yourself and meet me at the other end,' Mona shouted, pointing to an opening at the other side of the clearing.

Bram shuffled quietly with his back against the border, hoping to avoid the attention of the elves. He trod carefully and tried to keep his eyes open . . . but it was too painful. Ahead of him, an elf locked eyes with him and waited for him to blink – a sign that he was ready for a fight.

The harder Bram tried to keep his eyes open, the worse the urge to blink became, until he had no choice. The

instant his eyelids closed, the elf shot
towards him with a spiked net.

Bram yelped in fear, before running off
into the depths of the maze.

Alone.

Chapter 12

FULL MOON MAGIC

Bram was lost.

'Mona? Sheila? Tony? Bryan?' he called out. But nobody answered. He ran up and down between the towering hedges, trying to remember the way he had come, but everything looked exactly the same. 'Oh, devils, oh, devils, oh, DEVILS!' Bram whispered to himself.

As he rounded a corner, he heard the pummelling noise of footsteps ahead.

Bram pressed himself firmly into the hedge, trying to ignore the pain of the twigs poking into him.

The Overlords skittled past him one by one and didn't even glance in his direction, or notice that he was there.

'Oh no, they're ahead of us!' Bram cursed. *I'm going to be the one to ruin it for the team, aren't I?* he thought. *The Cereal Killers will never talk to me again.*

Bram continued to search the maze frantically for an exit. But the further he wandered, the more lost he got. He ran down lanes filled with ominous shadows and bounded along paths covered in gigantic footprints. His spine tingled at the claw marks that were dug deep into the earth, and he hoped to never bump into whatever creature had made them.

As he turned a
corner, his nose smashed into
something solid which almost knocked
him off his feet. In front of him stood
an enormous leg, and as his head tilted
upwards, Bram's eyes locked with the
menacing face of a *dragon*. He threw his
hands over his head, expecting to be
burnt to a crisp, but it didn't breathe out
a jet of fire . . .

It winked.

'Wandering stranger. What brings
you here?' it said. Its scales shone in
the moonlight, as if it were made of
glistening gemstones. But when Bram
took a closer look, he realized they
weren't scales at all. They were tiny,

delicate feathers in icy shades of blue.
Its eyes were as bright as the moon itself
and its claws were sharp enough to tear
through Bram with a single swipe.

'AHHHHH!'

Bram screamed as he tumbled backwards.
'Please don't hurt me!'

'I wasn't planning on it,' the dragon
said, chuckling.

Bram tried not to think about the
dragon's jaws chomping him up for
dinner. 'Do . . . do you know which way
I should be going? I'm . . . lost.'

'No, I cannot help you,' replied the
dragon.

Part of Bram wanted to run as far
away as he could – but something inside
told him to stay. 'Are you real? Or am I
already dead?' he asked.

'Yes, I'm real.' The dragon laughed.

'*Wow*. Dragons are some of the greatest villains of all time! I thought it was just a myth that you lived in the Wicked Woods and protected the school. It's an honour to meet you.' Bram beamed.

'Thank you. Are you a villain too?'

Bram shook his head. 'No. I'm not much of a villain.'

'I don't believe that for one second, dear boy,' said the dragon. 'You're only what you believe yourself to be. If you look deep within, I believe that you'll find confidence, courage . . . and the sprinkling of magic that makes you *you*.'

Bram shrugged. 'I doubt that. I'm not very confident or courageous.'

'I'm not so sure that's true,' the dragon replied.

'I don't have many strengths. My teachers think I'm stupid. I guess I can hear pretty well, though.'

'That's a good skill to have. I'm sure you have lots more. You just need to search inside yourself. Maybe then you'll find your way out of here . . .'

Just at that moment, the clouds parted and moonlight flooded the maze. A full moon sat, proud and glowing, in the night sky. His parents had always told him that he would feel at his baddest on a full moon, but Bram had never felt anything.

Until tonight.

Thinking back over his first week at Villains Academy, Bram realized he *had* been bad. He had broken into Master Mardybum's office. He'd confronted his friends – even Mona, who was slightly terrifying. He'd fought off the bindweed and a furious elf in the maze (well, he'd escaped them). And here he was with the courage to talk to a real, live dragon! He didn't care what anyone else thought of him – he *was* a villain! He *was* bad!

As the realization dawned on him, Bram's fur began to prickle and his throat began to fizz. He thought about his teammates. His new friends. He wished more than anything to escape from the Mystery Maze with them so one of them could win Villain of the Week and prove to the school and their parents that they *all* had what it took to be bad.

Bram's heart was filled with so much joy that he couldn't hold back the fizzy feeling bubbling in his throat any longer. He planted his feet firmly into the ground, looked directly at the full moon and let out a humongous

HOOOOOOOOOOOO
OOOOOOOOOWl!

It echoed through the night, reverberating around every hedge in the maze. His fur was prickling even more now, and suddenly out of nowhere it began to glow. The howl went on and on *and on* . . . until Bram felt like he had released all of the self-doubt that had built up inside him.

'I've never done that before!' Bram cried, his fur glittering a luminous green in the dark.

The dragon beamed. 'I think they heard you.'

From around the corner of the maze, Bryan came pounding towards Bram with Mona, Sheila and Tony on his back. 'That was some howl!' Mona said with a smile, as Bryan skidded to a stop.

'You're glowing. *Literally*. Are you wearing glitter? Also, there's a massive

dragon behind you,' Sheila said, sounding slightly afraid.

'I know,' Bram said, laughing. 'Isn't it amazing?'

'Come on, we can still win if we hurry,' Mona said and pulled Bram up on to Bryan's back. 'I haven't seen a flame in the sky yet, so the Overlords must be stuck too. What do you think the final part of the maze will be?'

'Master Mardybum's final words were: "Remember you're a villain". Do you think that means anything?' Mona asked.

'Maybe.' Bram shrugged. The cogs in his brain began to whirr as he thought back to all of Master Mardybum's lessons.

'Are you okay there, glitterchops?' Sheila asked, noticing Bram concentrating hard.

'What has Master Mardybum been saying all along?' Bram said. 'He's been telling us that we're not good-enough villains and to keep our enemies close! So *who* is our biggest enemy?'

'Erm, Master Mardybum?' Tony replied in confusion.

'No! Ourselves. We're our own worst enemies because we don't believe in ourselves. We don't believe we're villains.'

'Nice theory,' Mona said. 'But how does that help us get out of the maze?'

'We have to believe that we're villains!' Bram beamed.

Mona sighed. 'I'm not so sure about—'

But Bram cut her off. He opened his mouth and began howling.

'I AM A VILLAIN! AWOOOOO!'

Bryan laughed and joined in.

'I AM A VILLAIN!'

Soon, the whole group were screeching that they were villains. Bram's fur shone brighter and illuminated their whole surroundings.

'Come on, Mona,' Bram encouraged.

'I AM A VILLAIN!'

Mona shouted with glee.

Behind them, the dragon grinned. 'Congratulations, Cereal Killers. You've worked out the *true* purpose of the maze. You're now free to leave.' The dragon stretched out its feathered wings and revealed a beautiful stone archway behind it.

The Cereal Killers looked at Bram in awe and disbelief.

'We *are* villains.' Bram winked.

But as they left through the archway, a showering blaze of fire filled the air, along with cheers of success.

They were too late.

Chapter 13
VILLAIN OF THE WEEK

Master Mardybum stood in the clearing surrounded by the Overlords. As the Cereal Killers approached, he gave Bram a respectful nod. 'Well, I must say, I didn't think you'd be out so soon.'

'Never underestimate a villain,' Bram replied.

'Touché. Though you were still too late. The Overlords are the winners of the Mystery Maze.'

The Overlords sneered at the rest of the group. The Tooth Hairy grinned, Spike snapped his jaws as Jeeves rode up and down on them like a see-saw and Mr Toad burped loudly.

'But where's Mal?' Mona asked, looking around for him.

Master Mardybum began to look around too. 'Oh, yes, where is the boy?'

The Tooth Hairy looked nervous.

Mr Toad burped.

'Now, Mr Toad, I know that you ate a lot of the creatures and monsters in there, and I highly commend you,' Master Mardybum said, praising him, 'but please don't say you ate the poor boy too?'

'Of course I didn't,' Mr Toad ribbited in annoyance. 'I'm not a monster.'

'Then where is he?' Master Mardybum asked. 'Or does he not believe that he's a good-enough villain to get out of there? In which case, he can stay.'

'No, he believes in himself. But we lost him,' the Tooth Hairy whispered. 'He's still in there.'

Sheila cheered.

'DOES THAT MEAN WE WON?!

OH MY BADNESS!

WE WON! WE WON!'

'No.' Jeeves frowned. 'We were the first to make it out. *We* won.'

'Those weren't the rules, Jeeves. I told you that *every member* had to make it out of the maze. It's with deep condolences that I declare the Cereal Killers the winners,' Master Mardybum said.

The Cereal Killers whooped and hugged each other in glee. Mona shook Tony up and down, causing his bones to rattle in victory. Sheila flew through them all, giving everyone a head rush. And Bryan let off the loudest fart in excitement. 'It's all the nerves! It's just too much!' he said in his defence. Bram stood grinning at his teammates. He felt alive! His body tingled with elation. They had actually WON!

The Overlords were furious. 'What about Mal?' Spike asked. 'Is someone going to get him out of there?'

'Oh, yes, I suppose so.' Master Mardybum shrugged. 'Let's just give him five more minutes to find his own way out, though, shall we?'

'Excellent plan.' Mona grinned.

'And I suppose I should announce the winner of Villain of the Week too.'

Sheila eyed Master Mardybum and put on her baddest face. Tony smoothed out his cape. Bryan shook his mane so it appeared fluffy. And Mona looked bored with a hint of annoyance. Bram straightened his posture and squared his shoulders.

Master Mardybum looked at them all. There could only be one winner. The answer was clear. 'The winner of Villain of the Week is . . .'

'BRAM!'

'WHAT?!' Bram gasped in disbelief. He couldn't have heard it right. He couldn't be Villain of the Week, not after everything Master Mardybum had said and done to him!

The Cereal Killers dived on top of him, squeezing him in delight.

'You little—' Sheila started.

'How on earth did you beat me?' Bryan growled.

'Maybe I can kill after all?' Tony wondered.

'Congratulations!' Mona beamed. 'You deserve it, Bram. Really you do.'

'But why me?' Bram asked Master Mardybum, trying to make himself heard through the commotion.

Master Mardybum shrugged. 'Because you proved me wrong – and that is the sign of a true villain. Though, this does *not* mean that I like you. Now, I think it's about time we went to bed. I've had enough of all of you for one day.'

'But, sir, what about Mal?' the Tooth Hairy insisted, glancing at the maze.

'Oh, yes. The boy. I'll send one of the dragons in for him. That'll give him a fright.' Master Mardybum yawned and began walking back towards Villains Academy.

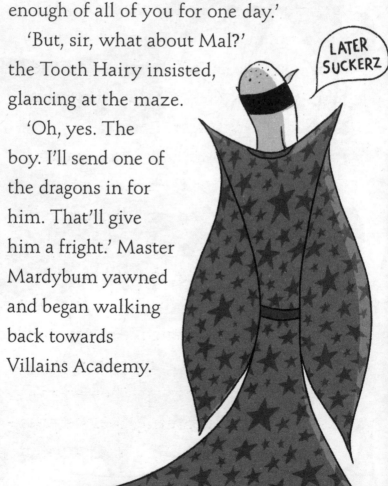

The team were on cloud nine-zillion as they walked through the misty grounds. The feeling of victory was glorious!

Whilst the rest of the students and Master Mardybum had gone back to their dormitories, Mona had asked the other Cereal Killers to follow her because she had a surprise for them.

'Will you officially share a dormitory with us now, Mona?' Sheila asked.

'If Bryan stops farting, I'll consider it,' Mona replied.

'I swear, it's all the cheese.' Bryan sighed with a lick of his lips. 'I just can't stop myself from eating it. Things should be a bit better now I'm not eating any more Furyflumps, though.' But Bryan's bowels were still emitting foul stenches, even without the Furyflumps.

Sheila patted his shoulder. 'Don't worry, my furry friend. We'll get through this together.'

The group laughed.

'I still can't believe Master Mardybum made me Villain of the Week,' Bram said in disbelief. 'He hates me!'

'He doesn't hate you. He was just pushing you. We all were,' Mona replied.

Bram smiled. He had never felt better in his life. He was surrounded by supportive friends and they'd all proved that they were bad enough.

In the distance, Mona's campervan came into view, but it was concealed by woven vines that rose from the earth.

'What's happened to your van?' Tony asked.

Mona smiled. 'It's had a makeover.'

With a click of her fingers, the vines
unwound and sank back into the earth,
revealing Mona's campervan. But it
looked . . . different. The bodywork
had been painted a black so deep that
it blended into the night sky, the moon
window had been revamped with stained
glass, and there were neon, multi-coloured
letters painted on the side that read:

THE CEREAL KILLERS.

'For all our future villainous road trips,' Mona said with a smile.

Sheila burst into tears, Tony and Bryan rushed over to see the paintwork, but Bram hung back. 'Does this mean we're proper friends now?' he asked Mona.

'Allies . . . maybe,' Mona jested and punched his arm softly. 'Don't make me hurt you. Come on, let's have a look!' Mona ran off towards the van and pointed out the spiked wheels to an excited Bryan.

Bram looked on from a distance with a massive grin on his face.

Maybe, just maybe, his time at Villains Academy wasn't going to be so bad after all. Not now that he had his friends around him, anyway.

Life was always better with friends, and being bad had never felt so good!

ACKNOWLEDGEMENTS

Being bad is a full-time job, but I'm lucky to have the most supportive and amazing team around me. There are lots of people I'd like to thank, so bear with me and don't switch off – or else . . .

Firstly, I'd like to thank my agent, Lydia. It's because of you that my dream became a reality, and I don't think I will ever stop thanking you. So, thank you for being the best agent ever.

Secondly, thank you to the team at S&S. I'm beyond grateful that you took the Cereal Killers into your hearts and enrolled at Villains Academy. Making a book is a massive team effort, and I'm thankful for every second that all of you have given me. Thank you to my editors, Ali and Amina – you are truly magical. Thank you to Sean for your support and design eye. To the rest of the team – Rachel, Laura, Dan, Ellen, David, Sophie, Jane, Dominic and everyone in between, thank you for being badass.

A big theme in Villains Academy is how life is better with friends and family, and I couldn't have done this without those amazing people around me. Thank you to my mum and dad for being the best. To Nicola, Brad, Gracie, Luke, Caron, Martin, Jim, Maureen, Emily, Anna, Hannah, Sarah, Megan, Iqra, Asmaa, Liz and everyone I've forgotten. Thank you for supporting me. And to my dog, Jack, who I lost whilst writing this book. Thank you for being a source of chaos and the bestest friend.

Thank you to Lowri, my biggest champion, friend and all-round amazing human being. I know you'll be thrilled to get your own line here, and I'm so grateful for your long texts and wicked humour – you are definitely a true villain.

As many people know, there isn't just one of me – I actually have a clone (well, twin brother). You won't be surprised to learn that I was always called the evil twin when we were growing up (sadly, I'm not kidding), and if I'm being honest, I don't know how anyone copes without a twin or without a Jamie. Thank you, Jamie, for always listening to my ideas for hours on end. I am so lucky to have you in my life, and I'm beyond grateful for your honest feedback, laughter, kindness and creativity.

Most villains also have a partner in crime, and I'm lucky to have Mitch as mine. Thank you, Mitch, for keeping me sane and believing in me from the start, even before I knew it myself. Words can't describe how much your love and support means to me. You bring out the best in me . . . and sometimes the worst when you snore. I don't think I could have done this without you. Love you lots.

Thank you to Sheila, the imaginary ghost in my family home, for your wonderful name and for scaring the bejeebies out of me.

A MASSIVE thank you to all the booksellers, librarians, teachers, authors, illustrators, parents, adults and children who have supported me and this gang of misfits. I am truly grateful to you and you make this job beyond enjoyable.

Finally, to all the weirdos and people who feel like they don't fit. You are my people, and you make the world a better place. Never let anyone tell you that you can't do something, and if they do, there are many things you can say to them.* Now go out there and be just a little bit **BAD**.

*Some examples are 'Go away' or 'Bog off', before you get any *bad* ideas.

WHO IS RYAN HAMMOND?

Ryan Hammond is an author, illustrator and book designer. He likes cute animals, quirky characters and VILLAINOUS traits.

He currently lives in Sheffield in an extremely haunted house, surrounded by lots and LOTS of books. *Villains Academy* is his first book.

HOW TO DRAW BRAM

1.

Draw a circle.

2.

Add ears.

3.

Add eyes, a nose and a mouth.

4.

Add the swirls of Bram's hair.

5.

Add strands of hair below the swirls.

6.

Add fur all over.

7.

Draw a body and arms.

8.

Add legs, feet and hands.

9.

Colour in for a woolly jumper effect!

And there's a villainously good audiobook too . . .